THE
BELL LADY
OF
BLAIRMONT
MANOR

Novella Jean

Copyright © 2022 by Novella Jean
Published by Crestmore Publishing LLC

ISBN 978-1-959385-00-4 (Paperback)
ISBN 978-1-959385-01-1 (Hardback)
ISBN 978-1-959385-02-8 (Kindle Ebook)

Cover design by Hannah Linder Designs

The Bell Lady
of Blairmont Manor

Deep in the wooded hills she roams,
  wandering with her bells.
You had better heed her warning,
  or else be damned to hell.

That jingling in the distance,
  those chimes you hear in the wind,
that is how she lets us know
  that evil still lurks therein.

So when speaking of Blairmont Manor now,
  you will hear the locals say,
"If you hear the bells, turn around,
  and run far away…"

1

TO THIA, EVERY DETAIL OF BLAIRMONT MANOR WAS perfect, and nothing could cast even the faintest of shadows on her vision of what it would become. Even the monstrous wrought iron gate at the entrance, which had originally been built as a show of importance and power, and which the residents of the small town of Daffodil regarded as a sign to stay away, seemed inviting and welcoming to Thia. If she bought the property, she would keep the gate open, but in that moment, pulling up to the entrance of Blairmont Manor at the end of the secluded mile-long road that led to it, through her windshield she admired the gate's beauty and strength, despite its ominous and intimidating design. She envisioned a string of lights along the top of it and along the wrought iron fence to either side, adding a jovial feel to soften its grandiosity while highlighting the elegance of the intricately decorated antique posts.

She turned off her car and got out, walking directly up to the gate. She tried to open it, but it was locked, so she looked through the iron columns and marveled at the magnificence of the mansion beyond, set back far enough from the road to be private but still partially visible. The driveway to the house began at this gate at the end of the road, but the entire road, all the way from its beginning at the small town square a mile away, might as well have been a private drive. Along its entire length, there were no other houses or buildings, only a dense forest filled with deciduous trees on either side for as far as she could see, a natural wall separating the estate from civilization that was, she would later find out, mutually designed to encourage both the outsiders to stay out and the insider to stay in.

Fall would be here before she knew it, and Thia imagined the woods abundant with the bright colors of changing leaves. She imagined the breathtaking and dramatic effect the drive up to Blairmont Manor would have on her guests, how the welcoming forest of calm and natural beauty would prepare them for a relaxing stay.

It had been her dream since childhood to run a bed and breakfast in a historic house, preferably in a quaint small town with locally owned restaurants and shops and loads of local charm. As she grew older, her dream changed from a small bed and breakfast to a boutique hotel, preferably in a converted historic mansion with enough land for recreational use, such as hiking, biking, and non-motorized water sports if there was access to a lake. This was the sixth house on her list of more than a dozen places to view before making the decision on which one to buy. With seventeen en suite bedrooms on nearly five hundred acres of land, which included a private lake, and being located only a mile from the most adorable historic town square she had ever seen, Blairmont Manor met all her criteria. As a plus, it was only a forty-five minute drive from the city and airport, making it convenient for special events and destination weddings.

She walked back to her car and pulled out her notebook to make notes while she waited for the realtor. Unlike all the belongs to Daffodil. A little more than a century ago, the town council bought it."

"Interesting," Thia said. "What are the plans for it?"

"There was an ordinance created when they bought it stating that it was never to be developed or changed in any way."

"How wonderful!" Thia replied, happy that her desire to keep the forest intact was a law. "So it's like a huge public park."

"Something like that," Carol said, "but people rarely venture into these woods."

When Carol did not explain any further, Thia asked, "I was also wondering about the land, nearly five hundred acres, right?"

When Carol nodded her head, Thia continued. "I'm looking for a mansion to convert into a boutique hotel, so I was thinking it would be nice to put trails in the forest for my guests to hike or maybe clear part of it and plant an orchard or vineyard they could enjoy as well. Have the owners ever had the soil examined, or do you know of any restrictions the town has for use of the land?"

"Where everything is now," Carol stated, "the forest, the area that has been cleared around the house, and the gardens, are exactly as they have always been since the manor was built in the late eighteen hundreds. To my knowledge, no previous owners have ever even looked into changing it. I expect it will stay exactly as it is forever."

"Oh," Thia said, surprised. "Well, I would want to have some experts come out to see what my options are. I guess I would need to contact the Daffodil town council about any changes I would make?"

"That would be wise of you," Carol said.

"And this fence," Thia started, pointing at it, "does it surround the entire property?"

"No," Carol said. "It extends roughly fifty yards to either side."

Thia wrote "fifty yards each side" next to her note about the fence in her notebook.

After an awkward moment of silence, Thia said, "Well, those are the only questions I can think of for now. I'm sure I'll have more once we get inside."

"Are you sure you still want to see it? It sounds like it might not be ideal for you if you are looking for a property with hiking trails and orchards and vineyards. I don't know if the Daffodil town council would approve those changes."

With a shrug, Thia said, "Since I'm here, I might as well look at it."

"Right," Carol said. She took a deep breath, pulled a large iron key out of her purse, and then used it to unlock the gate.

Thia smiled as she watched Carol insert the key into the lock and turn it, a loud clanking sound indicating the gate was now unlocked. "Now *that's* a key. Is it the original one?"

"Yes," Carol said, handing it to her. "It would be yours if you decide to buy Blairmont."

Thia held it in her hand, feeling its weight and admiring its ornate design. "It's heavy. What if I need another one? Or a locksmith? Can anyone even open a lock like this?"

"There's a guy in town who can do it. I'll give you his name if you decide to buy."

As Thia handed the key back to Carol, she said, "I would probably get it changed so it opens electrically. I'm surprised the owners never did that."

"For any questions on that, you would need to contact the town council," Carol stated.

"Oh," Thia said, again surprised. "I didn't think there would be restrictions on something like that."

"There aren't," Carol said, "but it would still be wise to contact the town council about any changes you would make if you decide to buy."

"Right," Thia said. In her notebook, she wrote "contact Daffodil town council about changes" on the fifth line.

There was another awkward moment of silence after Thia had finished making her note, as Carol remained motionless. Thia looked at the closed gate and then at the house beyond.

"Can we go see it?" Thia asked.

"Of course," Carol said. She waited a second before inhaling sharply and turning around to push the gate open.

Thia got into her car and drove through the entrance, with Carol following behind her. After driving along the portion of the curvy driveway that was still surrounded by forest, she reached the edge of the clearing and saw the entire house in all its breathtaking splendor. It was absolutely stunning. Just by itself, the mansion, made entirely of limestone, alone was an architectural masterpiece of majesty and grandeur. But combined with the well-maintained, beautifully designed gardens, the backdrop of the forest, and the southern Appalachian Mountains in the distance, it was almost too much for Thia to take in.

She followed the teardrop driveway and parked in front of the large veranda. Unable to take her eyes off the house, she felt for her notebook in the passenger seat and got out of her car. Carol pulled up behind her and turned off her engine. Thia did not mind that Carol did not get out of her car right away and took the liberty of walking up the stone stairs to the stone veranda. She tried to open one of the large wooden double doors, but they were locked. Feeling foolish, she turned around and waited for Carol, who was still in her car, her face looking downward and her lips moving. While she waited, Thia tried to peer inside the house through the windows. When she heard Carol's car door shut, she walked back to the top of the stairs to meet her. Carol suddenly looked at one of the windows on the second floor. Thia instinctively turned her head up and back to see what Carol was looking at, but the roof of the veranda obstructed her view.

"Perhaps we should look at the grounds first, while it's fresh on our minds," Carol suggested.

"Yes, of course," Thia said. "Good idea." She had been so distracted by the house that she had forgotten they had been talking about the land and her plans for it.

She joined Carol at the bottom of the stairs. As Carol led her along the driveway that jutted off of the teardrop formation in front of the house and wrapped around to the side, going through a porte cochere, Thia saw that it then veered to the right and continued on to the old carriage house. In her notebook, next to the note that read "gatekeeper's house," Thia added "and carriage house." Then, looking at the woods between the driveway and the carriage house and seeing that it was close to the house without disrupting the view and beauty, she added, "parking lot next to carriage house?" with a question mark to remind herself to speak with someone about clearing that land as a possible location for her guests to park their cars.

Instead of following the driveway to the carriage house, Carol led Thia on a path to the left that led to the gardens on the lakeside of the house, which were even more gratifying than the gardens in the front. There were already designated walkways, but Thia envisioned little alcoves with bistro tables and chairs for guests to sit and eat or have a drink while they looked at the lake and the mountains. The lake's shore was not as far from the house as she had thought it would be. The gardens, large and grand, extended to about halfway between the house and the water's edge. Between the gardens and the lake was a flat lawn with luscious green grass. As they walked toward that perfect lawn, Thia envisioned weddings, holiday picnics, and cocktail parties with the backdrop of the lake and the mountains in the distance.

And as for the lake itself, it was big but calm and still, perfect for families and even small children. She followed the water's edge with her gaze over to where the carriage house was located and saw a dock. Though empty at present, in her mind she saw canoes and paddleboards resting on the shore next to it for her guests to use.

"This is incredible," Thia said.

Carol continued to lead her along a path until they came to the edge of the garden. "We'll stay off the grass, if you don't mind," she said.

Thia came to a quick halt, having been just about to take another step to go down to the lake.

Thia turned around to look at the house, and her breath was once again taken away by its beauty. The facade, while fitting with the style of the rest of the house, was completely different from the front but equally, if not more, impressive. From where she was standing, she could see that the front and back gardens were continuous, wrapping around the side of the house opposite of the side where they had walked. She gazed at the manor, now eager to go inside.

But Carol was still facing the lake.

"Okay, well, I think I've seen enough," Thia said.

Turning only slightly toward her, not enough to see the house, Carol said with immense relief in her tone, "You have?"

"I meant of the outside," Thia clarified. "Can we go in?"

With hesitation, and Thia thought perhaps a hint of disappointment, Carol said, "Yes, of course."

They entered through the lakeside entrance, and Thia had to take a moment to adjust to the overwhelming intricacies of the interior. From across the floor, up the walls, and across the ceiling, not an inch had been spared in artistic design and detail. It was like no other mansion she had seen so far.

"I'm not sure Randy told me the right price," Thia said. In her mind, she was calculating what the actual asking price must have been and how much it would cost for her to furnish it, for a house such as this one would require only the most unique and extravagant furniture. In fact, all the pieces she saw there currently looked as if they had been specifically designed and made for this house. She also estimated in her mind how much the upkeep would cost, how much she would need to charge for guests to stay at such an exquisite hotel, and whether there was a market big enough for that price range. Having done extensive research, she knew an estate such as this one was above the threshold for the customers she had originally had in mind. People who could afford to stay in a place like this would expect amenities on the level of the most exclusive hotels in the world.

It was a beautiful mansion, for sure, but Thia felt disappointment as the logistics slowly crushed the emotional attachment she had already formed for Blairmont.

Thia continued, "I'm afraid the price he told me is well below market value."

"No," Carol said, "he told you the correct asking price. The owners are eager to sell."

Thia turned to her and said, "Then it must require some costly renovations."

"No," Carol assured her, "the estate has been very well maintained."

Thia began walking through the grand hall, Carol nervously glancing around them as she followed a few paces behind her.

So far, Thia had already begun researching retailers for furniture, and she had planned on getting contracts with local establishments for the complimentary toiletries and bottles of wine she wanted to provide for her guests. Now, she began to adjust those plans in her mind and envisioned designer furniture, high-end amenities, spa services, and other ways to please her newly targeted market for the luxury boutique hotel this manor demanded to be.

After a few minutes, they had reached the front entrance, and Thia had convinced herself that this would work. Her marketing plans would need to be only slightly altered—the targeted clientele for guests staying overnight would need to be set at a higher income bracket—but she could see this as her home and hotel. And as for her original market, it could still be targeted by opening part of the house for daily tours and hosting private events. Eventually, she could open a wine tasting room if she got a vineyard established and a restaurant if she hired a chef and staff. She was shocked it had not already been declared a historic building and put on the national registry and opened for tours. She was shocked she had been living in the nearby city and had never even heard of Blairmont Manor. This house was truly a gem that would not stay so well hidden for long, and she began to feel the pressure and urgency, knowing she had to pursue this now before the next person came along and saw all this unused potential.

Suddenly, a door slammed somewhere above them on the second floor.

Carol yelped, and Thia looked at her.

"Are the owners here?" Thia asked.

Carol quickly composed herself and said, "No, but it's probably just the housekeeper."

In her mind, Thia reviewed her memory of the driveway. She had not seen any other cars. But she had been so taken with the house and the property, perhaps she had been too distracted to notice. Or maybe the housekeeper had arrived while they were in the gardens.

"Anyway," Carol said, putting a hand on Thia's shoulder and ushering her toward the front doors, "I have a meeting I need to get to."

"Well, I was hoping to at least see the bedrooms, since that's where my guests would be staying," Thia said. "And the dining hall, since that's where my guests would eat. And the kitchen to see what kind of condition it is in now. And the ballroom and sitting rooms and the rest of the house, of course."

Leading Thia to those two grand wooden double doors at the front entrance, Carol said, "We can book another appointment if you need more time. Or, if you would like to get an inspection done, you can come back when the inspector is here." They exited to the front veranda. As Carol locked the doors behind them, she added, "It would probably be better because the inspector could answer all your questions related to converting this into a hotel."

Then Carol quickly descended the stairs and got into her car. Thia took a moment to walk around the veranda to continue looking at the property.

From her car, Carol said, "I need to lock the gate." She glanced up at that window again, and again Thia instinctively looked up to see what Carol was looking at but was unable to see through the roof of the veranda.

Then, Thia said, "Sorry, I forgot," and rushed down the stairs and got into her own car.

As Thia drove back to the gate, Carol following behind her, she was getting the feeling that Carol was not taking this showing seriously. It was only then that she realized Carol probably did not know her financial situation. Randy usually discussed the financial details with the selling agents. To Carol, a girl in her late twenties showing up alone at a house like this one was probably just curious or looking for good material for her daydreams. She had not even asked Thia if she was pre-approved for a loan or if she had investors or any questions on what kind of financing she was considering.

When Carol got out of her car, leaving the engine running, Thia parked and got out to talk to her.

As Carol closed and locked the gate, Thia said, "I don't know if Randy told you, but I will be making a cash offer."

Carol's eyes widened. "*Cash?*"

"I don't plan on getting any financing."

Carol tried not to look perplexed.

"You see," Thia explained, "this has been my dream for a *really long* time. I promise I'm not rushing into it. I majored in business in college with a minor in hospitality management, and right out of college I got a job with one of the most famous luxury hotels in the country. I've been working there and have learned so much, but I want to branch out on my own with something that is much smaller and more intimate, where I as the owner am present and involved with the guests. I've reached out to investors over the years since graduating, but no one would take a chance on me, and I never found anyone I wanted to partner with. So, when I won the lottery, I decided it was time to take the plunge."

"You won the lottery?" Carol asked, taking a genuine interest. "That's so cool! I've never met anybody who won the lottery before."

"Well, it wasn't the big one, but it was more than enough to take care of me and my family and to get this business going. I know everyone says never to invest your own money in your business and that it should probably be a sign that no investors gave me money in the past, but that was because I had no record and no experienced partners. They all said my pitch and my plans were solid but that I was too much of a risk for them to take on at the time. But I'm not a risk for me to take on because I'm ready and I know I can do this."

"So you've probably already bought a big house of your own. Have you done a lot of traveling? It must be nice not to have to work." Carol was truly curious and much more relaxed now, almost like a totally different person than the one Thia had met not half an hour earlier. Maybe, Thia thought, she could convince this new Carol to let her back in the house, now that she knew Thia was a serious potential buyer.

"No, I still live in my apartment in the city. I still work at the hotel, too. I'm getting great experience, and I want to stay on good terms with my boss and the other managers so I can call and ask for advice when I need it." She quickly added, "They know I plan on leaving as soon as I find a good location, though. And I have to say," she said with a wide grin, looking at the house, "I have found it."

"You really think you might choose Blairmont?" Carol asked.

"Yes, I do. I'm not just saying that."

"Are you sure?" Carol asked, though she could sense how serious Thia was.

"I am," Thia said with determination.

"And you would keep your apartment in the city and live there?"

"No, I plan on living at the boutique hotel, to be on site all the time, kind of like a glorified bed and breakfast, I guess." She gave a slight, awkward laugh. She could not stop looking at the house, so excited was she with the feeling that this was it, that she had found the location for her dream hotel.

Carol's eyes again widened, but instead of surprise, this time her expression was one of horror. She quickly glanced at the gate and then back at Thia. "You mean once you have guests staying there, too, right? But until then, you probably want something closer to town. I'd be happy to show you some places. Actually, there's a house I know you'd love that's about to go on the market."

"No," Thia said, shaking her head. "I plan on moving in right away so I can be on site and available twenty-four-seven to get the business going. There will be contractors, painters, movers, decorators, and so many other workers that I'll need to be available at all times. It doesn't make sense to live somewhere else while I'm converting the mansion into a hotel." Thia glanced down the road and added, "And anyway, it's only a mile. It's not that far from town."

Carol again glanced at the gate and then started slowly walking away from it, toward their cars. Lowering her voice, she said, "But don't you think it would be better to have a home away from your work, somewhere you can go and relax at the end of a hard day? Somewhere to go when you don't want to think about work?"

Thia followed her the short distance she had walked and also lowered her voice, though she did not understand why they had suddenly started talking like this was a secret. "But that's just it," Thia tried to explain. "To me, this isn't work. It doesn't feel like a job. It's fun and exciting, and I know I won't ever want to get away from it. Even now, on my days off, I still check in with my crew and others at the hotel, not because I'm worried or feel like I have to but because I genuinely love what I do." Thia knew from experience in trying to explain this feeling that it was difficult for a lot of people to understand.

"But when it's under construction," Carol suggested, "you wouldn't want to stay here during all that."

This woman really wants to sell me two houses, Thia thought, assuming Carol was trying to get yet another sale on top of this one. To appease her, Thia said, "I'm happy to look at that house you mentioned, the one that's about to go on the market, but I just wouldn't feel right if I didn't tell you that I've already made up my mind about this. I plan to live at the property where I run my boutique hotel, from the moment the sale goes through."

"Sorry," Carol said, "I didn't mean to be pushy. I'm just concerned for your safety. A young woman in a large mansion all by herself—the workers will know you live there alone, so please, be careful."

"Thank you," Thia said, genuinely touched by her concern. "Are you from Daffodil?"

"Yes," Carol said, "I've lived here my whole life, born and raised."

To Thia, Carol's attitude was yet another reason to choose Blairmont. "See," Thia said, "I don't need to be worried because the people around here have given me no indication that they are anything but honest, caring members of the community, like you. I got here this morning and had breakfast at the cafe in the town square, and then I went to some of the shops. Every person I talked to was so kind and so friendly. This really is a great town."

"It definitely is, and we love visitors, so please come visit anytime. But maybe it's not the right place for your hotel."

"Oh, I know it is," Thia said decidedly, "because I have chosen Blairmont."

"But you have other places to view, right?" Carol asked. "I imagine you would want to look at multiple locations to see what your options are before making such a huge decision."

"I've seen others," Thia said, "and I *had* more on my list, but I don't need to see them anymore. Daffodil and Blairmont have captured my heart, and I can't imagine any place being more perfect or fitting than this one."

"Well, sleep on it and give yourself some time to think it through," Carol suggested.

"Trust me, I've been thinking about this for a *long* time. I know exactly what I want, and this is the only place I've seen that has everything I could hope for. You can expect to hear from Randy with an offer later today."

"Well, take your time," Carol said. "There's no hurry."

"I thought the owners were eager to sell."

"They are, but I don't think anyone will put an offer on Blairmont any time soon. So, please, take as long as you need to make this decision. Look at the other properties on your list that you haven't seen yet. And go back to the ones you've already seen, to be sure, before you decide on this one. You're putting so much into your business. You want to make sure it is exactly what you want and what will best meet the needs of your customers."

"Thank you," Thia said, again trying to appease Carol. She held out her hand. "And thank you for showing me the property."

Shaking Thia's hand, Carol said, "It was my pleasure. Good luck with your business, wherever you decide to go. Please let me know when you open. I'd love to come and stay."

"I will, thank you," Thia said.

They went to their respective cars, and Carol drove off before Thia had even shut her door, causing Thia to feel terribly guilty about having talked with Carol for so long. She hoped Carol would not be too late to her next meeting.

She pulled out her phone and wrote a text to Randy: "I want to put an offer on Blairmont Manor right away."

Just before sending it, however, she got out of her car and walked up to the gate and looked through it at the house again, more specifically at that window Carol kept glancing at, trying to see if she could figure out what had worried the woman so much.

But Thia could see nothing of concern. All she could see was the big, beautiful historic mansion that would soon be her luxury boutique hotel.

2

"THIS GATE!" THIA'S MOTHER EXCLAIMED AS THEY pulled up to it.

"Wait until you see the house," Thia replied, stopping her car and putting it in park.

When Thia got out to open the gate, her mother got out of the car, too. The moving truck was not far behind them. It slowly came to a stop behind Thia's car at the end of the road.

Thia pushed on the gate to open it, but it did not move.

"Luckily, I brought the key," Thia said, pulling it out of her bag. "I asked Carol to leave this gate unlocked, but I guess she forgot."

Thia's mother looked through the iron columns to see the portion of the mansion that was visible from where they stood. With a gasp, she asked, "Is that it?"

"Yes," Thia said, having unlocked the gate and pushing it open.

After they got back into her car and drove far enough along the driveway to see the house in its entirety, her mother said, "Thia, I want to close my mouth, I really do, but I can't. I *physically* can't. This place is gorgeous!"

As she had done the first time she saw Blairmont Manor,

Thia followed the teardrop driveway to the front entrance, pulling forward to leave enough room for the movers to park in front of the stairs.

The four of them got out of their respective vehicles—Thia and her mother from her car and the two movers from the moving truck—and all seemed to just stand there for a solid moment, their heads tilted upward, their mouths open, their eyes wide and darting around to see all the details and grandiosity, needing that solid moment to take it all in.

"*Wow,*" Thia's mother whispered.

Not taking her eyes off the house, Thia relaxed her shoulders as she closed her mouth and smiled, the satisfying reality sinking in. This was really happening.

She turned to her mother and the movers. "Shall we go in?"

They followed her up the stairs to the veranda, admiring the mastery of the stonework.

As soon as Thia opened one of the large wooden doors, she was greeted with the same nineteenth-century settee in the entrance hall that had been there when she first saw the house with Carol and later when she returned with the inspector.

She set her curiosity aside and turned back to open the other door so the movers could easily bring her things inside—not that they needed a large opening. Having lived in a small studio apartment, Thia only needed one truck, and it was barely full, even after picking up the rest of her belongings that were still at her mother's house from before she moved out. The largest item she owned, aside from her mattress and the bed frame they had disassembled, was a dresser from a supermarket that she had put together herself.

While she opened the other door, her mother rushed past her into the house, gasping as soon as she saw the grand entrance hall. She immediately started going from room to room, gaping at the sight of each one as she looked from floor to ceiling, her mouth widening each time her eyes gazed from downward to upward.

The movers followed, feeling a mixture of being impressed at the sight of the high ceilings and dread at the sight of so many stairs. They walked around the entrance hall and peered into the nearby rooms to assess the size of the doorways and devise a strategy for bringing in the contents of the moving truck. Assuming she had already hired another crew to move all the current furniture in, one of the movers asked Thia, "Where do you want us to put the rest of your things?"

While the men had viewed the few adjacent rooms for logistical purposes, and while Thia's mother viewed the rooms with excitement, Thia looked at the rooms with confusion. Everything was exactly as it had been when she first viewed the house with Carol and later when she returned with the inspector. The mansion was entirely furnished—and not only with the big items. Lamps, little porcelain figurines, books in the bookcases—the previous owners had left everything, it seemed.

"Ms. Watkins?" the man asked, Thia having been momentarily shocked.

"Sorry," Thia apologized. "These aren't mine."

Her mother returned to the entrance hall and said, "You didn't tell me it was fully furnished!"

Thia quickly gathered herself and remembered her plans to store her things in the servants' quarters and live there during the renovations, a plan which she had formulated when she finally saw the rest of the house with the inspector. To the movers, she said, "Follow me, please."

She led them through the kitchen to a narrow stairwell and to the second floor where the servants' quarters were located. These rooms, at least, were still empty, as they had been when she saw them before. "The boxes labeled 'kitchen' and 'dining room' can go in the kitchen. I suppose you can put everything else in here."

As they all headed back toward the truck, Thia called Carol and told her the previous owners had yet to pack their belongings and, assuming there had been some kind of misunderstanding, asked when they planned on retrieving everything. It was Thia's nature to always begin with giving someone the benefit of the doubt, but having already started negotiations with interior decorators, antique dealers, and designer furniture stores, she was planning in the back of her mind where she would put all these items and how she would charge the previous owners for storing all their belongings for them.

"Anything they left in the house is yours now," Carol told her.

"Excuse me?" Thia asked, astonished. A few forgotten items in an attic was one thing, but it looked like people still lived here. Granted, their taste was on par with the design of the mansion, but it was still too much. "I don't think you understand," Thia started to explain, about to tell Carol that they had left *literally everything*.

But Carol spoke before she could say more. "I do understand," she said, "because everything that is in the house now was there when the previous owners moved in, too. Most of it is original or was added in the early twentieth century."

Thia's mother stood near enough to hear the conversation. When she overheard Carol offering to contact the previous owners, she shook her head and mouthed, "No."

Thia gave her mother a questioning look before telling Carol, "That would be great. Thank you."

After Thia ended the call, her mother said, "Are you crazy? There must be at least a hundred thousand dollars' worth of antiques in here! And we've only seen a few rooms." Then, eyes widening and gasping as if the thought had just occurred to her, she exclaimed, "What if the entire house is furnished like this?"

"Mom," Thia said seriously, "I've already met with decorators and have appointments set up for them to begin furnishing the rooms. If this whole house is still furnished, it will take days to pack everything and move it all out. And what am I supposed to do with all these things? Store them? Sell them?"

"What's wrong with keeping it as it is now?" her mother asked.

"It looks outdated."

"It looks like a Victorian-era-themed luxury estate," her mother argued. "People would love to stay in a place like this. It makes your hotel that much more unique."

By now, they had made their way back to the entrance hall. Her mother sat on the settee near the front doors and said, "It's not like it's a bunch of old, rickety crap." Patting the cushion she was sitting on, she continued, "This feels like it was just reupholstered. It doesn't feel like anyone has ever sat on it."

Dragging an empty dolly behind him on his way back to the moving truck, one of the movers said, "If I hadn't been eavesdropping, I would have thought all this furniture was brand new, just like period pieces made for this house, you know?" He continued past them and out the front doors.

Just then, Thia received a text message from Carol stating, "I couldn't reach them, but I'm sure they would tell you to keep it all and leave everything exactly as it is."

Thia told her mother what the message said. She looked around her, considering the possibility. Everything *was* fitting and appropriate for a luxury boutique hotel. And the house had been originally designed for hosting wealthy upper-class guests, after all, including royalty and foreign ambassadors.

Thia's mother leaned back on the settee and put the back of her hand to her forehead. In her best rich-person accent, she said, "Please, Jeeves, send them away. I can't be bothered to see anyone right now. And bring me another glass of champagne."

Thia snorted. "And what country was that accent supposed to be from?"

"Who cares when you live in a house like this!" her mother exclaimed as she stood up and started to gape at the rest of the house, her eyes darting from the exquisite floors to the decorative walls to the elaborate ceilings.

Resolving to seriously consider the idea of keeping the furniture later, Thia giggled excitedly and walked over to join her. "It's magnificent, isn't it? Come on, I'll show you the rest of the house."

Thia started to tell her mother what little she knew about the original design and construction and the tycoon who had it built. The movers finished unloading the truck before she and her mother had even gone beyond the first hall. When they found her, she asked them if they wanted to join the tour, and they gladly accepted. She showed them the rest of the main part of the house: three stories, each with high ceilings, seventeen bedrooms, each with its own en suite bathroom, eleven additional bathrooms, a ballroom, a large dining hall, several sitting rooms, a two-story library, an office, a conservatory, and a grand total of twenty-six fireplaces. Like the sitting rooms next to the entrance hall, each room in the main part of the house was completely furnished.

"I feel like I've traveled back in time!" her mother exclaimed. "You have to keep it like this."

Thia looked around them, truly considering it, but then she remembered her vision and what she had wanted her luxury boutique hotel to be like. She had never envisioned anything like this.

They had finished the tour and were exiting through a back door to view the gardens and the lake. The movers thanked her for showing them the house, and after she paid them, they left for their next job.

Thia sighed, still distracted by the mansion being completely furnished. "What am I going to do with all this?" she asked her mother.

"You don't have to make any decisions right now," her mother said. "Let's get something to eat. Then we'll come back and unpack, and you can sleep on it."

Thia agreed, and they ate lunch at a cafe in the town square before heading back to unpack Thia's things.

Near midnight, after a full day of moving, unpacking, and exploring the house, they were both exhausted. Thia's mother, having declared an hour before that she was going to lie down "for just a second," was fast asleep in Thia's bed, still wearing her clothes.

Thia, however, wanted to shower before getting into bed.

As she was showering, the shower door rattled—just enough to be unnatural. The glass door being transparent, Thia could see she was alone in the bathroom; there was no one rattling the door, even though that was what it had sounded like. Still, she opened it and stuck her head out to see if anyone was there.

She closed the door and then quickly poked it, trying to replicate the rattling that had just happened.

But the door did not budge.

She hit the door with the side of her fist.

Nothing.

Then, because it was a door that fit securely in its frame, she grabbed the handle and shook it as forcefully as she could. Only then did a slight rattling occur. As soon as she stopped, the door was still. She shut off the water and watched the door for a minute, trying to think of what on earth could have caused it. Unable to come up with an answer, she figured odd noises and other seemingly inexplicable occurrences must have been part of living in a house that was more than a century old. There were probably tons of little quirks like this that she would have to get used to. She turned the water back on and finished showering before heading off to bed.

3

THE FOLLOWING MORNING, THE CAFE IN THE TOWN square was full of local townspeople, all amiable and cheerful. When Thia and her mother walked in, they got the looks of curiosity newcomers could expect in such a small town, but in the spirit of the community, they were not looks of disdain, but rather welcomed greetings of smiles and nods.

"Sit wherever you'd like," a server said with a smile as he walked by them.

They saw an empty table and headed toward it, receiving a few "good mornings" and nods from patrons already sitting and eating as they walked by occupied tables.

"I love this little town!" Thia's mother exclaimed as she sat down.

"Every person I've met here is friendly," Thia said. "It's one of the reasons I chose Blairmont."

At the mention of Blairmont, the man sitting at the table next to them turned and looked at her.

Thia and her mother smiled at him.

"Did you say Blairmont?" he asked.

"Yes," Thia said. "I just moved in."

"You plan on living there?" he asked.

"Yes," Thia replied. "I'm turning it into a hotel."

In response, he raised his eyebrows.

Thia continued, "You're welcome to come by and see it anytime, once it's up and running. I hope to get it registered soon as an official historic house and have some of the rooms open to the public for tours."

As she spoke, a look of consternation slowly formed on his face, despite his obvious effort to conceal it.

"I don't want to charge admission for the residents of Daffodil, though," Thia added, realizing she was sounding like a salesperson, when in actuality she was just excited. "I'm hoping it will be more of a service to the community, something to bring tourists here. And because it really should be open to the public. It's not fair to historians and architecture enthusiasts to hide a masterpiece like that. It's such a beautiful mansion, don't you think?"

"I've never seen it," he replied.

"You know it's just down the road, right?" Thia's mother asked. "You can see part of the house through the fence. It's *huge*. And gorgeous."

"Yes, you should come and see it once it's open," Thia added.

"Thank you, but I think I'll pass," he said. Then, before Thia could tell him the offer still remained if he changed his mind, he added, "You should, too."

Thia and her mother exchanged a look.

Turning back to the man, Thia started to say, "If you change your mind—"

"You should do yourself a favor and leave now while you still have your head above water." In response to the looks of offense from both Thia and her mother, he said, "I don't mean to be rude, just honest. It's good advice. If no one else told you that already, then I'm ashamed. You're not safe there."

"Why not?" Thia's mother asked, her expression having turned from offense to concern.

He hesitated, as if considering how best to say what he meant. Instead, he said, "I'm sorry, but it's not my place to say. I shouldn't have said anything. But good luck to you. I mean that. I really do wish you the best." With a sympathetic nod and downcast eyes, he returned his attention to his food and coffee and continued eating his breakfast.

Following his lead, Thia and her mother turned their attention back to each other. Thia looked at the menu and asked her mother, "What are you getting?" And they did their best to resume the morning with the same cheerful optimism they had shared since waking up at Blairmont.

A few minutes later, the man left, giving them a small smile and nod as he got up from his table.

Aside from that small, odd encounter, Thia and her mother enjoyed the made-from-scratch food and warm atmosphere of the small-town cafe where everyone seemed to know each other. The morning had returned to normal, and they had almost forgotten about the seemingly out-of-place manner of the man. But as they left the cafe and walked to Thia's car, they ran into Carol. After some small talk, she said to Thia as she walked away, "Give me a call when you decide to sell Blairmont, okay?"

Thia and her mother continued to smile and wave as they got into her car. Once the doors were shut and they were buckling their seat belts, Thia's mother said, "That was a weird thing to say."

"Yeah, she's kind of strange," Thia said as she turned on

the engine and started to drive. "When she showed me Blairmont, I *barely* got to see it—only the back hall to the front entrance on the first floor—because she had to leave for another meeting. Who schedules a showing for a place like Blairmont for only half an hour?"

"Real estate agents are always trying to make a sale as quickly as possible," her mother replied.

"But she acted like she didn't want me to buy it. She kept telling me to look at other places and to take my time."

"Do you think it's because what that man said is true? That it's not safe?" her mother asked.

"Carol did say she was concerned that people would know I live there alone. But other than that, I don't know why anyone would think it's not safe."

"Unless they know something you don't," her mother said, sounding uneasy.

"No, I'm sure it's just because I'm young and living by myself. But it won't be empty for long."

AS IT WOULD TURN OUT, THIA SOON DISCOVERED, the stranger at the cafe and Carol were not the only residents of Daffodil who felt like Thia did not belong there and who expected her to vacate the premises sooner than later. Upon returning home after driving her mother back to her house in the city, Thia was forced to stop at the closed gate at the entrance, park her car, and get out. Looking around to see if anyone else was there, she walked up to the gate and pushed on it to open it. The gate, however, did not budge. Thia pushed harder, but it was locked. She looked through the iron bars down the driveway. A car was parked under the porte cochere, headlights facing the entrance, indicating the driver had reversed back into the spot.

"Hello?" Thia yelled, but there was no one in sight.

She pulled out her phone and called Carol.

After exchanging pleasantries, Thia said, "I remember you mentioned a locksmith in town who could open the gate to Blairmont. Can I get the number? I seem to be locked out." She tried not to sound annoyed. More than anything, she was confused. She had left the gate open when she and her mother had left early that morning.

Carol gave her the number, and Thia had just dialed it when she saw a woman leave the house through the side door under the porte cochere.

Thia ended the call and yelled toward the woman, "Hello!"

Seeming not to have heard her, the woman continued into the car, started it, and drove toward the gate. If Thia had not been so distracted by the occurrence of a stranger having been in her house, she would have noticed that the woman also seemed confused, although not surprised, that the gate was closed and locked. She stopped her car and put it in park, leaving the engine running, and stepped out, large iron key in hand.

"Hi," Thia said with a smile.

"Hello," the woman said as she began unlocking the gate on her side. "Can I help you?"

"I'm Thia, the new owner."

Having unlocked the gate now, the woman began to swing it open, saying, without looking at Thia, "Nice to meet you. I'm Millie, the housekeeper."

"Oh!" Thia exclaimed. "Carol told me about you. She said you've been the housekeeper for years."

"My whole life," Millie said. "I helped my mother and grandmother when I was a child, just as my daughters and granddaughters help me now."

"Good, I'm glad to hear you have help," Thia said. "It's too big of a house for one person."

"It is," Millie agreed. "There are some others who drop by sometimes to help, too."

"Well, I'd love to talk with you," Thia said. "Do you have some time now?"

"Sure," Millie said, not moving.

"Do you want to come back to the house?" Thia asked, thinking she would put on a pot of hot water and they would sit down and discuss the arrangement over tea. It was all she could offer since she had not had time to make sweet tea or get food from the store.

"No, right here is fine," Millie said.

"Oh," said Thia, slightly disappointed. "Okay. Well, I would love to keep you on as the housekeeper, of course. You know the house much better than I do. But I wanted to discuss schedules, rates, and staff. I'm turning Blairmont into a hotel, so I'll be hiring additional housekeeping. Not that I don't think you could handle it," Thia added, not wanting to offend Millie. "You do an excellent job. It's just that with a constant changeover of guests, there will be a lot more cleaning to do. I was thinking you could help train the new staff and maybe even take on a managerial role. What are your thoughts on that? It would be more pay, I'm sure. How much do you charge?"

"Nothing," Millie replied with that "bless your naive little heart" look. "I work for the house."

Confused, Thia said, "I own the house," thinking Millie must have been misinformed about the arrangement of the sale. "There's no trust or estate to pay you from. If there was one before, from which you were compensated, there's not one now." She quickly added, "I'm happy to pay you, though, of course. I just don't know what your rates are."

"Nothing," Millie said again. "I've never been paid to take care of Blairmont, nor was my mother, nor hers before that. It's just what we do. We've been charged with taking care of it—cleaning it, inspecting it, maintaining it, fixing whatever wears out or breaks, replacing whatever becomes too old to function." In response to Thia's obvious confusion at this setup, Millie continued, "This isn't my day job, which is why I keep odd hours. I'll drop by a few times a week, when I can. If something needs to be fixed, I'll have someone come out and fix it." She said this with a matter-of-fact tone that told Thia she need not worry about anything, that Millie would handle everything, as she always had.

"Thank you," Thia said, "but I will be hiring a housekeeping staff. I suppose you won't need to come by anymore, once I've hired people, but I'd be happy to have you on my team. Like I said, you know the house better than anyone, so I'd be indebted to you. And, of course, I want to pay you for your work."

With a tone that indicated she was only saying these words because Thia wanted to hear them, and as though she did not believe it would actually happen, Millie said, "Sure, I'd be happy to train your staff if you hire anyone. I'll still stop by and keep house when I can, though. My daughters and friends may stop by, too." As she started walking to her car, she said, "If you need to reach me for any reason, Carol can give you my number. Otherwise, maybe I'll see you next time I drop by, if you're around."

Thia followed Millie to her car. By this time, Millie was

already sitting in the driver's seat and was about to leave. Thia leaned toward the door, and Millie rolled down the window, her eyebrows raised in expectation. "Is there something else?"

Thia replied, "I left the gate open when I left this morning. I'm going to keep it open from now on. There will be a lot of contractors and workers coming before I open the hotel, and then there will be guests, so it just makes sense to keep it open."

When Millie only glanced at the gate and then back at Thia, eyebrows still raised, Thia said, "I can take your key so you don't have to keep track of it anymore."

"It's no trouble," Millie said. "I'll hang on to it, just in case. I suggest you keep your key with you at all times, too, in case you get locked out again." Then, she added, so softly that Thia barely heard it, "Or locked in."

She put her car in drive and drove off, swerving around Thia's car that was parked just outside the gate.

Thia watched as Millie's car got smaller in the distance, baffled, if not slightly creeped out, by the encounter and that last little comment about getting locked in.

She returned to her car and drove to the house, leaving the gate open. Inspired by Millie, she parked under the porte cochere to use the side door. Upon entering, immediately to the right was a door to the kitchen, disguised as part of the wall when it was closed. Beyond that, the large hallway was lined with large squares of dark cherry wood adorning the walls, each square carved with designs. As she walked on the hardwood floor beneath her, a small echo could be heard with each step. She stopped in the middle of the hallway. The echoing stopped, too. She stomped one foot down and heard the echo reverberate along the walls and up to the high ceiling above her. She looked up and stomped again, amused at the sound of the echo. *Fascinating*, she thought. After one more stomp, she turned and continued down the hall to the main entryway.

She set her tote bag on a table and pulled out a pen and her notebook. Turning to the first blank page, she started making notes on changes she might make. Going down the halls and looking into the rooms, she envisioned which ones would be open to the public, which wings would be reserved for guests staying at the hotel, and what kind of signage she would use to indicate these rules. She planned to do this daily, knowing she would change her mind several times before making any final decisions. She was still considering the furniture—the more she looked at each room, the more she liked the idea of keeping everything as it was.

When she had finished going through the first floor of the main part of the house, she sat at the large antique desk in the office to write more notes. She then turned to her page on restaurant ideas and wrote down potential interview questions for the executive chef position. She made additional notes on what she needed to look up in terms of licenses and permits. And on a new page, she wrote down a few items she already knew she would need, such as new mattresses, new linens, and outdoor furniture she wanted to put in the gardens.

As she wrote these notes, out of the corner of her eye she thought she saw one of the drawers of the desk *slowly*—so slowly it was barely noticeable—being pulled out. It was not the sight, however, that had caught her attention so much as it was the slightest, barely audible sound of the wood of the drawer scraping against the wood of the desk.

Thia looked down at where the noise was coming from,

and indeed the drawer was pulled out nearly an inch.

Brow furrowed in confusion, Thia leaned down to get a better look. As she inched her face closer to the drawer, she could have sworn she heard the low chuckle of someone laughing under their breath right next to her. She quickly sat up and looked around the empty room and then toward the doorway.

"Millie?" she yelled in the direction of the rest of the house. Then, thinking it may have been one of Millie's daughters or someone else who might still have access to the house, she stood up and asked, "Hello? Is someone there?"

She walked toward the doorway, and as she did so, she heard footsteps echo behind her. And yet, these echoing footsteps were not like the ones she had found so amusing in the hallway earlier.

She stopped and turned around.

The echoing footsteps stopped, too.

She turned around and started walking toward the hallway again.

The echoing footsteps started again, sounding like someone was walking behind her.

She stopped.

The echo stopped.

She turned around to face the room again and stomped.

Another stomp—not hers, and not an echo either. No, it was another stomping sound, a single thud of a shoe hitting the floor, not the fainter sound of a reverberating echo.

Thia stomped again, looking at the spot on the floor several feet away where she had heard the sound of the other stomp, the one she had not done herself.

After a deliberate pause, she heard another stomp, the sound coming from exactly where she was looking, yet she was alone in the room.

Again, that low, nearly silent laughter.

To the empty room, she asked, her voice quiet and unsure, "Hello?"

Silence.

She asked again, more sure of herself this time, "Hello?"

Silence.

She stomped again and listened for a responding stomp.

Silence.

She stomped again.

Silence again.

She thought about the shower door rattling the previous evening and then about Millie saying that she, her mother, and grandmother had watched over this house. Considering all the repairs that must have been done over the years, she would likely discover odd little things like this each day, as pieces of the house of various ages adjusted to the seasonal weather. In fact, she now thought, it was probably not a stomp she had heard but rather a crack or popping sound from some part of the house expanding or contracting with the change in temperature.

She sat back down at the desk and, just prior to returning to her notes, looked down at that drawer again. It was closed.

With all the thoughts swimming around in her head, from thinking about the business to thinking about how big and old the house was, she now wondered if she had imagined the whole incident of the drawer being pulled out—and of the shower door rattling the previous evening, too.

I need a break, she thought, convinced her mind was just tired from thinking of the business for so many hours without rest or interruption.

Deciding that grocery shopping would be the most productive way to take her mind off of her work, she closed her notebook, retrieved her tote from the table she had set it on, and went to her car. Then, after buckling her seat belt, she unbuckled it and went back inside the house to get the large iron key to the gate, just in case.

On her way out, driving down that secluded one-mile road, she passed a truck headed in the direction of her house. Thia turned her car around and followed it back to the entrance, where the truck stopped and an old man got out, large iron key in hand, to unlock the gate.

Thia pulled up next to the truck and immediately got out, too, putting her car in park but not turning off the engine. She grabbed two iron columns and shook the gate with all her might.

"Excuse me, miss," the old man said, politely positioning himself closely beside her without bumping into her so he could insert the key. "It's locked."

"Who locked it?" Thia asked, almost accusingly.

He looked at her with a stern, grandfather-like look of reprehension at her tone and audacity. "Well, I don't know. Could have been a number of people. What business do you have here?"

Realizing he did not know who she was—nor she him— Thia remembered her manners. "I'm sorry," she said. "I was just so distracted by this gate being locked. I *just* left, and I left this gate open." She held her hand out toward him. "I'm Thia, the new owner."

At the mention that she was the new owner, the man's expression softened. He shook her hand and then turned back to the gate. As he unlocked and opened it, he said, "Nice to meet you, Miss Thia. I'm Herschel, one of the groundskeepers. I say 'one of' because I'm too old to do all this by myself, so I get help, mostly from my great-grandsons these days."

"Right," Thia said, recognizing the name. "Carol told me about you." She was still too distracted by the gate to bring up all the business she had wanted to discuss with him—his rates and schedule and working with a crew she would hire, basically all the same business items she had planned on discussing with Millie.

She pulled the gate shut, thinking it must lock automatically upon closing, but when she pushed it again, it opened.

Turning to Herschel, she asked, "How did this gate get locked after I left?"

Herschel frowned and said, "Someone must have locked it if you didn't."

"But there's no one else here," Thia said. Then she looked beyond the gate, toward the house, and asked, "Right?"

Then, she looked at the gatekeeper's house.

Right? she asked herself again in her mind.

She walked to the gatekeeper's house and tried the door.

It was locked.

She went to her car and turned off the engine. Taking her keys from her tote bag, she looked on her keychain for the one to the gatekeeper's house as she walked toward it. After finding the right key, she unlocked the door and went inside. The little three-room cottage was empty.

She climbed the small narrow staircase to the sleeper loft.

It was empty, without any sign of anyone having been there.

When she walked down the stairs, Herschel was in the cottage, looking around. "It's been forever since I stepped foot in here."

"It appears it's been forever since *anyone* stepped foot in here," Thia said. Unlike the main house, the gatekeeper's house had been neglected over the years. The outside was fine and beautiful, but the inspector had pointed out many parts of the interior that would need to be fixed before she could allow guests or staff inside.

"Well, I have work to do," Herschel said as he left.

Following him, Thia said, "Actually, if you have a minute, I'd like to discuss the terms of your employment. I understand you've been the groundskeeper for a long time, and I'd love to keep you on, but I was never told your rates or schedule or anything."

"We don't have to discuss any of that. I work for the house, so you don't have to worry about a thing. I come when I can, usually with the boys, so you'll see us from time to time. We'll stay out of your way."

"I don't know if anyone told you, but I'm turning Blairmont into a hotel, so I will need to hire an additional crew. But I was hoping we could work something out, since you know the grounds so well and since you've worked here for so long."

"Sure," Herschel said, like he was appeasing a toddler who had asked him to ride a pretend unicorn with her, "we can do that."

Feeling another Millie situation coming on, Thia said, "No, really, I want to pay you and either have you be part of the staff or maybe train the staff I hire."

"We'll cross that bridge if we get to it," he said, walking back to his truck.

Thia sighed internally. "Okay, well, I also wanted to let you know that I want to keep the gate open from now on. I'll be hiring a lot of workers who will be constantly passing through this entrance, and then there will be guests, so it's easiest to just keep it unlocked and open."

With a smile, Herschel said, "Okay," and got into his truck and drove toward the house.

Thia watched his truck go down the driveway, feeling heavy with the knowledge that—like Millie and Carol and the man at breakfast that morning—Herschel did not take her seriously in the slightest. And that they all seemed to assume, for some reason or another, that her presence there was temporary.

4

WITHIN THAT FIRST WEEK OF LIVING AT Blairmont, Thia found out that seeing the property, having it inspected, and moving in were easy by comparison to actually getting settled. She knew starting the business would include a learning curve, even with her knowledge, training, experience, and education. But she had severely underestimated the ease at which simply establishing herself would be, both in terms of the house and the town. That first full day at Blairmont had been only the beginning of the resistance she would face, not only from Millie and Herschel but from every local townsperson. Everyone in Daffodil was sociable and eager to get to know her as the newest member of their community—until she mentioned Blairmont. Once she mentioned where she lived, every single person would shift their demeanor, even if only slightly, and they would take on an air of distancing themselves from her, like a wall had suddenly dropped from above to separate them as soon as the word "Blairmont" was uttered.

And as for Millie and Herschel, and whoever came with them to help with their duties, they did not seem to regard her as present in the house at all. When she had returned from the grocery store, all the furniture she had rearranged had been put back to their original positions. When she confronted Millie about it later, Millie shrugged it off and told her she would be "wise to keep everything as it is and stick to the servants' quarters." When she asked Herschel about the soil and planting an orchard or vineyard somewhere on the property, he said everything was "just fine the way it is." Her notebook, in which she kept all her notes on the business—notes from phone calls, business cards from vendors, and her ideas—kept disappearing. And the gate was not only closed but also locked every single time she had to pass through it, whether leaving Blairmont Manor or returning.

On top of all that, she had overestimated her own capability of living alone and away from the city, not being surrounded by people as she was used to, living in an apartment downtown and working at a busy hotel.

So it was no wonder that she was eager to fill the house with people as soon as possible. It was why she had decided to keep all the furnishings the previous owners had left behind and to do only the most necessary renovations. It was why she had already bought and washed new sheets, pillowcases, and comforters to accompany the mattresses and pillows she had ordered. And it was why she had invited all her sorority sisters from college to stay for a weekend later that month—and why she was nearly beside herself with excitement when eight of them said they would come. Just one friend, one familiar face who knew her and to whom she did not have to explain herself, would have made all the difference in the world, but to have eight of her closest friends coming was one of the greatest pleasures she could look forward to. It breathed new life into the house, now that she could imagine specific people seeing it for the first time.

Already the mansion seemed less ominous, and already she felt less lonely, just knowing they were coming.

Thia stood at the water's edge, the gardens and Blairmont Manor behind her, the lake before her, and the foothills beyond. The mountains appeared to have a bluish tint, like there was a filter over them, the slightest differences in shades outlining the ridges. It was one of those "false fall" mornings of early September—she knew better than to think the cold weather was there to stay and that it was truly autumn just yet. Hot days would return. But this was the first morning in months that actually felt cold instead of the usual cool-yet-muggy feeling. The thick layer of dew that normally covered the grass at sunrise had been replaced with frost, and a light fog was hovering just above the lake.

She pulled out her phone, brought up the tracking website, and refreshed the page to see if the status for her expected delivery had changed. The latest update for her pillows and mattresses still read, "Out for delivery." She checked her recent calls, but there were none that she had missed.

Pressing the button on the side of her phone to turn off the screen and focus on the beautiful scenery that surrounded her, she slipped off one of her shoes and dipped her toes into the water. Immediately, the icy sting caused her to reflexively pull her foot back. The minnows she had been watching scattered, and she slid her toes back into the water, just beneath the surface. She watched through the water as she nudged a small rock with her big toe so that it slowly floated above the other rocks before settling several inches away. Then, pulling her toes out of the water, she slipped her other shoe off and settled her feet firmly on the cold grass, letting the soft blades chill the soles of her feet. Closing her eyes and hugging her arms around herself, she inhaled deeply through her nose, letting the cool sensation of the crisp air fill her lungs. And as clear as the air and as real as the beauty and nature that surrounded her, she heard a woman's voice whisper in her ear, "You will never succeed."

Startled, Thia's eyes shot open, and she immediately turned her head to look in the direction of the voice, wiping her ear as she did so, for she was convinced she had even felt the hot sticky breath of the words, as if the person who had said it had been standing so close to her that their shoulders should have been touching.

But there was no one there.

Instead, in the distance she saw Herschel walking briskly, half running, toward her.

Slipping her shoes back on, she started walking toward him and shouted, "Good morning!"

He did not respond but only continued with that brisk, intentional stride, a man on a mission.

When they met, she opened her mouth to speak, intending to invite him inside for coffee and breakfast, but before she could get a word in, he admonished her for being on the grass and asked if she would kindly stick to the walkways in the gardens. It was not the first time he told her to stay off the grass, and he was clearly disgruntled at having to tell her more than once.

Thia took a deep breath, controlling her rising temper at his complete disregard for her ownership of the property. With a small smile and a small apology, she explained that she liked to admire the lake up close.

As he put an arm around her shoulders and led her back to the gardens, Thia made a mental note to figure out a gentle way to tell him she planned on allowing her guests to walk on the grass whenever they pleased, not to mention weddings and picnics.

ONCE THE DELIVERYMEN HAD REMOVED ALL THE OLD mattresses, put the new ones in place, and left, Thia spent several hours putting all her new pillows, sheets, and comforters on the beds. She stored the old linens in the smallest bedroom, which she planned to use as a storage closet. To make room for more items that would be stored there in the future, she pushed the small bed into a corner and relocated the other pieces of furniture to various rooms in the house. She then drove to the city to run some errands and have dinner with friends.

When she returned, she went straight to her room in the servants' quarters and retrieved her pajamas and toiletries to take with her to one of the main bedrooms for the night. She wanted to stay in each bedroom at least once before opening the hotel to paying customers so she could see for herself that each room was satisfactory, and now that there were new mattresses and linens, she felt comfortable sleeping in the beds.

Upon entering the first bedroom, however, she was overcome with frustration, though she knew she should not have been surprised. The linens had been changed back to the original sheets and bedspread. She checked the bedroom next to this one and the one across the hall. They, too, had been changed back to the original linens. Thia set her toiletries and pajamas on the chaise in the corner of the bedroom she intended to sleep in that evening and went to the small now-storage room to get her new sheets. Upon entering the small room, however, she immediately saw that it had been restored back to its original look and layout, the furniture she had moved out of the room having been moved back in. And her new sheets and comforters were nowhere to be found.

When she had first ordered the pillows, sheets, and comforters, she had stored them in this small bedroom while she waited for her new mattresses—only to later discover that they had been moved to a room in the servants' quarters. Suspecting that was where they had disappeared to this time as well, she switched off the light before going to that part of the house and found them there. She gathered one set, carried it back to the bedroom where she planned to sleep that evening, and changed the sheets.

As she did so, she practiced conversations in her head on how she would address this issue with Millie. Having been so educated in the hospitality business, she had been trained in conflict resolution, but those courses and seminars always assumed the dispute would be between other people, the opponents likely being employees under her management or patrons of the establishment. But this situation with Millie was entirely unexpected and unknown to her. She needed to figure out how to establish boundaries and demand respect, if not at least acknowledgement of ownership. Yet, she also needed to maintain good relations. Millie was a well-known and well-respected member of the Daffodil community—a community to which Thia was still so very new that most of its members either did not know who she was or were inclined to immediately dislike her upon finding out where she lived. It would be a great advantage to be in good favor with Millie when talking with other residents of the town and trying to fit in. Additionally, Millie did her a great service by helping her take care of the house while she worked on finding and hiring a full-time housekeeping staff. And Millie had done a splendid job in the past in the upkeep and maintenance of Blairmont Manor, to which Thia was indebted because it was in such an extraordinary condition that she was substantially ahead of schedule in terms of opening her luxury boutique hotel. She decided she would call her former boss the following morning and ask for advice on the issue. Hopefully, together they could come up with a solution that would please both Millie and Thia.

After she changed the sheets, changed clothes, and brushed her teeth, Thia went around the house checking the doors and switching off the lights, as she did every evening. And when she checked the small storage room, which was now back to being a bedroom, she searched her memory for assurance that the light was supposed to already be off. She was certain she had turned it off not an hour ago, after looking there for the new sheets. But it was on. Attributing the lapse in memory to distraction and fatigue, she switched off the light, and as soon as the room went dim, she saw someone move near the opposite wall.

She quickly switched the light back on.

There was nobody there.

Still, she walked across the room to where she thought she had seen the motion near the servant door that was disguised as part of the wall when it was closed. The door led to the network of hidden passageways that had been included in the floor plans of the house so the servants could conduct their duties and move throughout the building mostly unseen. The hidden servant doors had a handle on the side of the hidden hallways, but there was no handle on the bedroom side so that the door was identical to the wall. Instead, there was a lever over the top of the door in the servants' hallway that forced the door open. The mechanism that activated the lever was disguised in the designs of the bedroom wall. Not knowing where the camouflaged activation mechanism was located but knowing there was one somewhere, Thia began pressing along the decor of the wall near the door, feeling for any movement. When she felt it, she pressed on a six-inch square, and the hidden door opened several inches.

Sliding her fingers into the space between the door and the wall, she pulled the door open and looked down the bleak, narrow hallway. Using the flashlight on her phone, she illuminated the dreary little hallway and saw nothing. She stood still, holding her breath, and listened. She heard nothing.

Stepping back, she shut the small servant door, restoring the wall to its intact and uniform appearance. She walked back across the room, switched off the light again, checked the room again, and saw nothing—no figure of a person, no silhouette, no indication of anything or anyone moving.

She sighed, convinced there was nothing of concern, and attributed the small incident to a trick of the light. Since taking up residence at the old house, she had learned that shadows and illusions often appeared at random because the millions of little designs and carvings in the walls, ceilings, furniture, and sculptures created a mixture of odd angles of light, comprised of different colors and luminosities. This was not the first time she had seen such an illusion, but it still sent a shock through her every time it happened.

She went back to that first bedroom where she would sleep for the night. By now a light rain had begun outside, the pitter-pattering against the windows creating a soft, harmonious ambience as she turned off the lights and slid under the covers. She settled onto the new mattress as it conformed to the shape of her body, enveloped by the smooth and expensive new linens.

Her guests were going to love staying there.

As she closed her eyes, she allowed the soft noises around her to lull her to sleep: the light rain against the window, the soft hum of the central heat and air, the soft thudding of movement in the third-floor bedroom above her.

Having lived in an apartment complex for her entire post-college life, a sorority house before that, and with her mother in the city before that, she had grown accustomed to the continuous sounds of other people, whether they were in the building or outside. If anything, those sounds were comforting to her.

But then Thia remembered that now she lived in a house—alone.

She opened her eyes and sat up, listening for more movement. Now, it sounded like there was someone in the hallway, just outside the room.

"Millie?" she asked in the direction of the open bedroom door.

She got out of bed and switched on the light. Then, she went into the hallway and found the light switch for the sconces that lined the walls.

Seeing no one, she stood still, listening for movement again. She heard nothing.

As she switched off the lights and returned to the bedroom, she made a mental note to hire an exterminator to check the house. She could not believe she had not already thought of that, but now she was convinced it was an animal she had heard. In the city, mice might live in the walls, but for all she knew, out here in the woods there could be larger rodents crawling around in this house.

With that thought in mind and a small shiver as she imagined a raccoon or an opossum roaming the halls, she shut the bedroom door behind her. As she headed back to bed, a slight irregularity in the wall caught her eye. The servant door was open, the smallest of space between it and the wall revealing the dark hallway behind it. Figuring she must have accidentally activated the lever on her way out of the room, Thia pressed on the door to close it and went back to bed.

She lay there, tucked in bed, in her safe little cocoon of expensive bedding in this luxurious mansion that would soon be her hotel, and she listened to the rain outside, focusing on how unique this time in her life was, hoping it would be the only time in her life that she would live alone like this.

And yet, somehow Thia felt like she was not alone in the bedroom. She heard no one and saw no one and had no real reason for it, but it just *felt* like there was someone else there, in the room with her. Maybe it was due to being in a different part of the house. Maybe it was due to loneliness and anticipation of the girls' weekend to come.

Turning on her side, she reached across the bed and turned on the small lamp on the bedside table. The hue of the light, softened by the greens and blues of the antique stained-glass lampshade, made the room oddly calming in how it distorted the colors of the wallpaper, curtains, comforter, and canopy. The air was still and undisturbed, and yet that odd feeling persisted, like there was space in the room being occupied by an additional presence that was not her own.

Propped up on one elbow, she lay on her side, completely still aside from her eyes moving to see about the room. If the heavy energy in the room were to be attributed to another being, she could not define its exact position.

Then, though it was barely audible, she heard what sounded like breathing, slow and rhythmic, like someone was snoring somewhere in the house. Yet, it was unnatural in its intentional timing, almost as if it were forced.

Shhhh . . . . . Shhhh . . . . . Shhhh . . . . .

She followed the sound with her gaze to the pillow next to hers.

Shhhh . . . . . Shhhh . . . . . Shhhh . . . . .

For several moments, she continued to watch the empty space, trying to think of an explanation, until she realized the rhythm of the sound matched the rhythm of her own breathing. She relaxed then, reasoning that it was probably some odd reverberation of her own breath, caused by the canopy over the bed or the carvings in the walnut bedposts or bouncing off the sheets because of the angle of her position.

Leaving the light of the bedside lamp on, she slid one arm under the pillow as she lay her head on it, and with her other hand she pulled the covers over her shoulder. In her effort to fall asleep as quickly as possible, she focused not on how desolate the old mansion felt now, but on how cheerful and lively her new home would be once it was full of guests.

5

CARLA AND GRETCHEN WERE THE FIRST TO ARRIVE,
and Thia had a pitcher of margaritas ready to pour for them
on the veranda. Nearly twenty minutes later, Renee's car
could be seen coming down the driveway, with Deidre in the
passenger seat. Drinks in hand, the four girls offered words
of congratulations and constant expressions of how
impressed they were with the manor. They decided to wait
until everyone was there to tour the inside and instead
stayed outside enjoying the scenery and fresh country air.
Upon receiving a text that the other four were stuck in
traffic, they went to the restaurant in the town square, where
they would meet Crystal, Monica, Valerie, and Ruth.

After dinner, Thia poured them each a glass of local wine
to drink while she gave them a tour of the mansion. One of
her goals while her friends were there was to get their
opinions on the local wines she had gathered from wineries
in the region, to help her choose which ones she would offer
her guests when she opened the hotel.

They started with the great entrance hall at the front,
and Thia told them what she knew about the original family
who had built the manor and that most of the furniture was
original. In the hallway by the kitchen, she pointed out the

echo effect, and for several minutes they had fun yelling, whispering, or singing and hearing the echoes. She showed them the door in the hallway that was disguised in the wall and explained that there was a whole system of hidden passages. When they entered the ballroom, they sang and danced and guessed how many pieces of crystal were in the chandeliers.

The girls marveled at each room, eyes wide and mouths agape at the splendor of all the details. Only Carla and Valerie exchanged looks at some of the oddities of the house, the little things that could be considered cool or creepy, depending on the tendency of the opinionated person. But when Thia opened one of the hidden servant doors and offered to show them the hidden hallways, Gretchen said, "Thia, you must be the bravest person I know for living here by yourself."

At that the other girls laughed and agreed—and politely declined her offer to explore the network of dark, gloomy, narrow little hallways that ran between the walls of the main rooms.

"What do you mean?" Thia asked.

Crystal answered for Gretchen. "Thia, this house is huge and beautiful, but isn't it at least a little daunting to be here all by yourself?"

"Not really," Thia said, closing the disguised door. "I spend most of my time in the servants' quarters or in the rooms near the kitchen. I only come over to the main wings of the house when I'm checking on things for the business."

"Still…" Monica said.

"It won't be empty for long," Thia said, leading them to the grand hall on the lakeside of the house. "Now that I've decided not to make any major changes, I'll be opening soon.

I'm planning on having some holiday events to attract attention and renting the ballroom, conservatory, and other venue spaces for parties and balls in the winter. Hopefully I'll be able to get some guests before that, but I'm sure by spring I'll have all the rooms booked through the summer. And by then I'll have daily tours, outdoor events, and maybe a restaurant, so there will be even more people here, not only overnight guests. Plus, with local staff commuting every day and seasonal staff living in the dorms, this place will be bustling with lots of people. Sure, it's a little lonely for now, but it's just for now."

They walked through the gardens on the lakeside of the house and out onto the lawn, where Thia had arranged nine wooden Adirondack chairs in a circle next to the lake. The sun had already set, so in addition to leaving on the indoor lights, she had turned on all the outdoor lights and lit tiki torches she had placed around the area where they would sit.

The humid night air was warm around them, and the girls sat in the chairs, pouring more wine as they continued chatting with each other. Listening to the beautiful fusion of people laughing around her and bugs chirping in the forest, Thia basked in this blissful moment of true happiness as she envisioned many more nights like this one. She was living the dream.

Then, a quiet moment occurred, one of those moments when one conversation has ended and the next has not yet begun, and Carla asked, "Does anyone else get...just, like...*vibes* from this place?"

Roughly half the voices that responded said, "Yes," while the others asked, in various ways, "What kind of vibes?"

"Just like...*vibes*," Carla said.

"That's literally what we just asked you to clarify,"

Deidre said, causing the other girls to laugh in response.

"I'm sorry, Thia," Carla said, "but this place is *creepy*."

"I agree," said Valerie.

"It's big and intimidating, I'll give you that," Monica said, "but it's only a big house. It probably just feels creepy because it's empty." Turning to Thia, she said reassuringly, "It's going to be awesome when you have the hotel going. There will be people everywhere, and there will be tons of good energy because people are always happy when they're on vacation. And being surrounded by all this beautiful nature is a wonderful escape from the pressures of life, very relaxing. Really, Thia, this is amazing, and we're all very proud of you."

All the girls agreed and lifted their glasses to Thia, who stood up and gave a small bow. Then, in seriousness, she lifted her glass and said a toast of gratitude, thanking them for coming and for their general support of her pursuing her dream.

After the toast, Gretchen said to Monica, "You're right." Then to Carla she said, "I thought the same thing earlier, about it being big and scary, but Thia's been living here, and nothing has happened."

"Well…" Thia started.

All the girls turned and looked at her, wide eyed, as if they had just been waiting for it this whole time.

"No," she started, shaking her head and waving a hand, "not like that, not anything big." She said no more, but when the girls remained silent, watching her, waiting for more, she said, "Just little things, here and there. Stupid things that shouldn't be a problem, but I'm still trying to figure out how to deal with them, you know what I mean?"

The girls were still silent, still watching and waiting for

her to elaborate. Finally, Crystal said, "No, we don't. What little things?"

Thia picked up a bottle of wine and went around the circle topping off their glasses as she answered. "First of all, there's this issue with Millie, the housekeeper, and Herschel, the groundskeeper..."

She told the girls about the gate constantly being closed and locked, despite her telling Millie and Herschel she wanted to keep it open. She told them about how Millie and Herschel insisted they worked for the house and would not let her pay them, how they insisted on keeping everything as it was when she moved in and put things back in their original places after she moved them, and how they never once acknowledged that she was now the owner. Then, she told them about how each townsperson she met was nice and agreeable, until she mentioned Blairmont Manor.

"I don't know if they hate newcomers or if the previous owners were snobby or what," Thia continued. She was back in her seat by this time, sipping her wine. "But I'm nice. Even if they didn't like the previous owners, it doesn't mean they won't like me. They don't even give me a chance."

There was a moment of silence, and then Thia added, "And there have been some noises, some creaking floorboards, popping or cracking sounds, probably just the house settling or materials responding to changes in air pressure."

A few of the girls looked at each other uneasily.

"Once, I could have sworn I saw a curtain move on its own. Another time, I was in the kitchen, and it looked like there was someone behind me in the reflection in the window. A couple of times, I thought I saw someone standing in the shadows."

Seeing the wide eyes of shock and surprise from the girls, Thia quickly explained, "It's an old house with old bones. And there are tons of lights at different locations, from floor lamps, table lamps, sconces, and chandeliers. They cast odd angles from every direction. And they're all different luminosities and colors from all the fabric or stained-glass lampshades.

"For example, one time I turned off a light and thought I saw someone standing in the room, but when I turned the light back on, I realized it was only a shadow from the huge grandfather clock. I realized that when I had turned one light off, a light from another room had caused an odd shadow to form, making it look like someone was there, when in reality it was just a different angle from the clock." She took a sip of wine.

"Or maybe I'm just seeing things," she continued. "Really, it's all fine. But you're right when you say it's scary sometimes to be in a place this big all alone—except I'm not alone because Millie and her daughters come and clean. But they're so quiet I don't even know they're here until I see that things have been moved around, while I was still in the house."

A few more uneasy glances were exchanged between the girls.

"And Millie has a handyman she hires to do repairs," Thia continued. "And they just show up whenever they want to, without ever calling in advance to tell me.

"Like this past week, I hired a crew from the city—I had to get a crew from the city because I couldn't find a single local who would do it. Anyway, I wanted them to install shelves and cabinets in the smallest bedroom because I want to turn into a storage closet—it's so much smaller than the other bedrooms, it just makes more sense to not even try to rent it out and is more cost effective to use it for storage. So, they worked on the room while I was cleaning up the old carriage house"—with a flick of her hand, she indicated the direction of the carriage house in the distance—"because I want to turn it into a dormitory for seasonal staff in the summers. And out of nowhere, the foreman sent me a text message saying he got spooked so they were leaving."

"Spooked?" Crystal asked. "What is he, a horse?"

All the girls laughed, and Thia continued. "So Millie said she could get her handyman to finish it for me. I said that would be great and asked for his number, but she wouldn't give it to me. I don't even have her number—or Herschel's. For some reason, neither of them will give me a way to contact them. So, I told her to tell him to call me. Then, I went out and ran some errands, and when I came back, she was still here and said he had already been by and finished the job. I asked how much I owed and how I was to pay him, and she said not to worry about it because he works for the house."

All the girls expressed various forms of agreement that this was truly strange.

Thia continued, "When I went to the bedroom, he had taken down all the shelves and cabinets the other crew had been installing, and it looked exactly as it had before."

"What?" all the girls exclaimed.

"I know!" Thia said, so happy to finally be able to vent about all of this. "So you see," she explained, "it's not that it's scary living here, it's just that there are all these weird little things." She took another sip of wine. Laughing, she asked, "Seriously, what am I supposed to do with these two old people who want to work for free and who are helping me take care of this huge mansion and who have done such a great job of caring for it for so many years—but who won't let me live in my own house the way I want to?"

The girls erupted with laughter at the situation.

"That is so awkward," Valerie said, wiping a tear from her eye, and all the girls agreed.

"So, what are you going to do?" Crystal asked, still laughing.

"I'm still trying to figure that out," Thia said. "I want to remain on good terms with them, but they aren't making it easy."

"It's *your* house," Renee said. "Tell them to hand over their keys and that you'll call the cops if they return."

"I may have to resort to that, but I really don't want to. I think they've been doing this for so long that it's not easy for them to adjust to a new owner, let alone it being occupied full-time and becoming a hotel. I get the impression that this was like a second home in the country for the previous owners. I don't think they were here that often."

"How old are Millie and Herschel?" Deidre asked.

"I don't know exactly, but Herschel is *really* old, as in so old that I'm impressed he can still do manual labor. He says his great-grandsons come and help him, but I've only ever seen him here by himself. And Millie's granddaughters help her around the house, but I have yet to meet any of them."

"Are you *sure* they have grandchildren?" Ruth asked jokingly.

"Yes, because despite telling Millie and Herschel I wanted to keep the gate open and change things in the house, the gate keeps getting locked, and things keep getting moved back to where they were originally. I think it's because Millie and Herschel didn't tell anyone else what I wanted. Like all this furniture out here"—Thia gestured toward the chairs they were sitting on and the items in the garden—"they put all this in the carriage house after I had it all set out, and I had to drag everything back out here today."

The girls laughed, and Thia continued. "I can't tell you how relieved I was when I saw that all the new sheets, pillowcases, and comforters were still on the beds after we came back from dinner because Millie keeps changing them back to the original ones."

"Maybe that's what she came to do now, but she's too busy watching us like a creeper," Carla said.

"What?" all the girls asked as they looked toward the house.

"What are you talking about?" Renee asked.

"See?" Carla asked, pointing at the house. "She's watching us from that room up there."

"Where?" Monica asked.

"Right there, in that window," Carla said.

"Which one?" Crystal asked.

"Yeah, there are like a hundred windows," said Deidre.

They had left all the lights on, so the girls' eyes were darting across the windows, looking for Millie.

"The one with the woman standing in it," Carla said, her frustration clear in her tone.

"Not helpful," said Gretchen.

"She just smiled and waved at us," said Carla.

"Smiled and waved?" Thia repeated. "That's not Millie. It must be one of her elusive daughters or granddaughters I have yet to meet."

Turning in her chair to bring her attention back to the circle, Valerie said, "That's so weird that they move things around while you're in the house without asking you."

The other girls turned their attention back to the group, too, and Deidre said, "I wonder why Millie does that."

Ruth said, "I wonder why any of them do it. And all for free? That's weird, too."

"So weird," Renee said, and all the girls, except Gretchen, agreed.

"How am I the only one who sees what's really going on here?" Gretchen asked.

"Since you're the only one, why don't you enlighten us?" Monica teasingly suggested as she poured herself another glass of wine.

"Ummm, obviously Herschel and Millie's sick, deranged, psycho love child lives in the walls of the house," Gretchen joked, causing all the girls to burst out laughing.

"I've never even seen Millie and Herschel interact," Thia said. "They're never here at the same time. I'm not even sure they know each other."

Gretchen continued, "Think about it. Mill and Hersch had a scandalous affair back in the day, and to cover it up, they kept him here. And now he's some middle-aged, forty-something-year-old freak who is unfit for society because he's *never* been allowed to leave the house. And they 'work for the house' because really they've been keeping him here and are still taking care of him. And those weird noises, those strange shadows, that person who keeps moving furniture while you thought you were alone in the house— that's all *him*. And you don't know it because he uses all those creepy secret passageways that the architect put in the house so the rich people would never have to see the help."

As she was saying this, all the girls were laughing so hard that most had tears in their eyes.

"Why would you say that about the house we're all about to sleep in?" Crystal exclaimed.

"No, I'm not sleeping here," Carla declared.

"Why not?" all the girls protested.

"This is too much for me," she said. "Can I borrow someone's car? I'll come back in the morning."

"You can't be serious," Gretchen said. "I was only joking."

"I'll drive you," said Valerie.

"What? You, too?" the girls asked.

"Seriously," Valerie said. "I know you were joking, Gretchen, but"—turning to Thia, she continued—"someone could be in the house, maybe not living there, but someone could totally be somewhere, in some room in some other wing, and you would not know it."

"Okay, can we change the subject?" Deidre asked. "I'm not going to be able to sleep tonight."

"You can all sleep in my bed," Thia offered, standing up. Having noticed they were running low on wine, she said, "I'll get us some more to drink. Does anyone need anything else?"

"I'll help," said Ruth, standing up to join her. "I need to use the restroom anyway."

On the way to the house, when they were far enough away that the others would not hear them, Ruth whispered to Thia, "Have you thought about seeing someone?"

"No," Thia said, "I can't think about dating right now. I have way too much on my mind."

"No," Ruth said, stopping her. "I'm talking about a professional. I know you have an explanation for everything going on, but it sounds like you're not sure. And stress can do strange things to the mind." Thia shrugged and opened her mouth to respond, but Ruth continued, "Let me give you my psychiatrist's number. She's amazing, and it has been such an incredible journey since I started seeing her last year. You've taken on so much, and you're all alone out here. I know it's difficult for you to relax because you want this hotel to be in business ASAP, but it's too much for one person. And you know we love you and support you no matter what, but maybe the stress is getting to you a little bit, and that's okay to admit. It's okay to take a second and assess what's going on in your life. It's okay to take the time you need to get it done in a way that keeps you healthy, physically and mentally."

"Thanks," Thia said, giving Ruth a hug.

"Promise me you'll at least consider it, okay?"

"I promise."

They went into the house, and while Ruth went to the bathroom, Thia got more bottles of local wines from the kitchen. Then, after a thought, instead of going through the back door, she used the side entrance under the porte cochere, where Millie usually parked. She exited the house and looked down the driveway. There were no cars. She walked to the front of the house and looked at the cars lined along the teardrop formation in front of the veranda. Thia saw her car, Gretchen's car, in which she and Carla had arrived, Renee's car, in which she and Deidre had arrived, and Valerie's car, in which she, Monica, Crystal, and Ruth had arrived.

Thia looked back at the house, an unpleasant feeling rising inside her as she considered the impossibility that one of Millie's daughters would have made it from somewhere in the back of the house, where she could be seen in a window from their location near the lake, to her car, and then drive off in the short amount of time it had taken Thia to come out here. She looked down the driveway through the gate, which was still open, and down the road. It was pitch-black, without any hint of red from taillights.

Still perplexed, she went back into the house and met Ruth in the kitchen, and the two girls carried more wine down to their friends. By the time they reached the circle, the girls had moved on and were gossiping about old acquaintances and telling stories. Well after midnight, Valerie and Carla left, and the remaining seven girls went to bed—but not before moving wardrobes and other large pieces of furniture in front of the hidden servant doors in their bedrooms.

The weekend passed without any of the unsettling events Thia had experienced alone. Although they returned Saturday morning, Carla and Valerie did not spend Saturday night at Blairmont Manor, either. The girls enjoyed the weekend, filled with laughter, swimming, and exploring the house and Daffodil. Most of all, they enjoyed just being together. For Thia, it was a much-needed, sweet taste of what life would soon be like once she opened her luxury boutique hotel.

6

"SO," MONICA'S HANDYMAN BEGAN AFTER examining a few of the hidden servant doors. He worked in the city but had agreed to come to Blairmont to help Thia upon Monica's request. Monica had given Thia his number with a glowing recommendation after Thia told her about how much trouble she was having finding anyone local to help her, and every person she had found who worked in the city said Blairmont was too far of a drive.

The two of them were currently in one of the bedrooms, with him standing next to the disguised door that he had just inspected. "I think the best idea would be to put a deadbolt lock in the door, with the deadbolt going into the wall to lock it. Or you could do a swing bar lock, which would include putting the swing bar on the wall"—he pointed at a location on the wall next to the door—"and the ball that catches it on the door." He pointed at the corresponding location on the door. "Both will stand out, so the doors won't be as disguised as they are now. But I can try to find colors that might blend in, or you could try painting them."

"And the deadbolts wouldn't have key access, right?" Thia asked.

"No, ma'am, not if you don't want them to," he said.

Thia was fairly certain she would turn the servant hallways between the bedrooms into closets, but until she had the actual renovations done, she decided to put locks on the doors—in case she booked the rooms before doing any construction or if she took Monica's suggestion to keep the hallways there for the hotel staff to use. Either way, guests would want to be able to lock those doors.

And she did, too.

Every time she looked at one of the servant doors in the wall now, she was reminded of the time she thought she had seen someone in the room and had just boldly opened the door and checked the servant hallway, taking for granted her certainty that she was alone. Looking back, she could see now just how dumb that had been to do. No, she did not think there could be one iota of truth to Gretchen's joke about the love child living there, but she had been naive to not even consider that someone other than Millie or her daughters could be somewhere in the house without her knowing it. Up until now, every time she heard someone in the house or when things had been moved around when she was supposed to have been alone, she had assumed it was Millie. Now, she literally shivered at the thought that it might have been someone unknown to her.

So in addition to locks on all the servant doors, she wanted locks to all the bedroom doors—to which she alone would have a master key—which guests would expect to have on the doors to their rooms anyway. And his suggestion of the swing bar lock sounded like a good idea for the main bedroom doors, too. She was also replacing the locks to all the external doors. If Millie and her daughters wanted to continue to come to the house, they would have to do so while she was there and inform her of their schedules. And she was having security cameras installed.

She told herself these were all business expenses because she would need them for the luxury boutique hotel anyway, but she knew the urgent rush to get everything done as soon as possible was for her own peace of mind while living there alone until the business was in full swing.

"Okay," Thia finally said after thinking it through. "How about for the hidden doors, we do deadbolt locks without key access. And for the bedroom doors, we'll do deadbolt locks with key access as well as swing bar locks as an extra security measure."

"Sounds good. How many locks will I need to get?" he asked her.

"I'll get the floor plans," Thia replied.

At the kitchen table, they leaned over the blueprints to Blairmont Manor and counted the number of bedroom doors, doors leading to the outside, and all the disguised servant doors. He left and purchased all the locks, returned, and then spent the remainder of the day installing all of them. Satisfied with his work, Thia praised him as she paid him and told him she wanted to eventually hire someone to be on call twenty-four-seven, in case he or someone he knew was interested.

"I plan on having living spaces set up in the old carriage house, and there's the old gatekeeper's house, too. It could be seasonal or year round," she told him, trying to make the job sound as appealing as possible.

"I don't think you'll have any problems finding employees," he assured her. "It's a beautiful house, out in the country, with a beautiful view."

"Thank you," she said, withholding her urge to tell him

the reason he was there was not because of his superior skills so much as it was because no one else would come. "But if you know anyone who might be interested, you'll tell them about it, right?"

"Sure, I'll spread the word."

"Thank you," she said.

After he left, Thia went around the house and made sure all the servant doors that had access to the network of hidden passages were locked. Then, she also locked all of the bedrooms.

The security company came the next day, and she had them install cameras throughout the house, a few outside, and one at the gatekeeper's house to cover the entrance. She was also able to find an electrician from the city to install Victorian-style lamplights above the posts at the entrance. And after many phone calls, she found a junk removal company that would remove the iron gate and take it away.

EVERY FIRST THURSDAY OF THE MONTH, THE Daffodil town council held a town hall meeting. Thia planned to attend every single one as a way to establish herself as a member of the community. She already made a point of shopping locally and eating almost every meal out so she could be seen and become familiar to the townspeople. The town hall meetings, she hoped, would further convince the community that she was there to stay.

The room was already packed, even though she had arrived early. As Thia made her way to an empty seat in the middle of one of the back rows, she received a few glances and saw a couple of people whisper upon seeing her. But for the most part, she was ignored. The town council members began the meeting with the upcoming Halloween Festival, and the person in charge took to the podium to update the audience on the budget, the committees, and the festivities planned. As the council moved on to discuss mundane details and general funding issues, Thia started planning in her mind how she could include the Blairmont Manor Hotel in the Halloween Festival. It was probably too late, given how far along the committee already seemed to be in their plans, but there was always the next year. And if Daffodil had festivals for every holiday, then she could probably talk with someone about Thanksgiving and Christmas. She was so distracted by her ideas that she was not paying any attention to the meeting, but her ears perked up when they casually mentioned they had received permission to use a portion of the "Blairmont Fund" to clear away some overgrowth in the forest along the town square.

Thia leaned toward the person sitting next to her and whispered, "What's the 'Blairmont Fund'?"

Without looking at her, they responded, "It's the money from the sales."

"What sales?" Thia asked.

"Blairmont. Every time it gets sold, the commission goes to the town to maintain the house and the area around it."

"Why?" Thia asked.

"That's the arrangement."

"They take the commission from all the real estate sales?" Thia asked with disbelief.

"Not all real estate sales, just every time Carol sells Blairmont."

"How often does that happen?" Thia asked.

"Every couple of years or so."

Eyebrows raised, eyes wide, and mouth opened, Thia was unable to hide her shock. But the townsperson with whom she had been speaking was no longer paying attention to her and continued to look straight ahead.

So distracted was she by this information that Thia barely heard what other matters were discussed. When the meeting was over, she worked her way against the exiting crowd to the front, where the council members were still sitting and talking at a long table.

"Excuse me," she said to get their attention. "I'm Thia Watkins, the new owner of Blairmont Manor."

They all greeted her with various forms of "hello" and "welcome" and "nice to meet you."

"What can we do for you?" one of the council members asked.

"Well, I originally came to ask about putting street lights along the road to Blairmont, as well as a sidewalk, and switching out the sign that says 'DEAD END' with one that says 'Blairmont Manor Hotel.' But I also want to ask about the 'Blairmont Fund.' Someone told me it's from the commission of the sale, and that it's used for upkeep of the house. Is that true?"

"It is," another council member said.

"But isn't that my responsibility, as the owner?" Thia asked.

"Yes, but in our experience the extra funds are necessary," the first council member said.

"As for the street lights, sidewalk, and sign," a third council member chimed in, "we'll send someone to talk about all that when you get all your permits and licenses."

"Yes," Thia said with a laugh. "You're probably familiar with all the applications I've submitted—business, overnight hospitality, home tours, food, alcohol, outdoor recreation—"

"They're still under review," the first council member said, cutting her off.

"I'm sure all the taxes and revenue the hotel will generate will more than pay for everything."

"We'll see," another council member said.

After the council members continued to look at her in silence, Thia took the hint that the meeting was over. "Okay, well, thank you for reviewing them, and please let me know if there is anything else I need to do," she said.

"We will," the first council member said with finality.

OVER DRINKS THAT EVENING WITH DEIDRE AND Gretchen, Thia told them about what she learned at the town hall meeting.

"What do they mean when they say they got permission to use the funds?" Deidre asked. "Permission from whom?"

"Sounds like some kind of Mob operation," Gretchen suggested.

"Right?" Thia agreed. "Am I being paranoid in thinking the town council is trying to sabotage my plans by delaying permit approval and not allowing locals to do any work at the estate because for some reason they use the selling of Blairmont Manor to generate revenue for the town? A business that is a hotel, an event venue, a historic house that offers daily tours, a restaurant, and hopefully someday a vineyard and winery is a much more sustainable method to generate revenue for the town. I don't get it."

"I'm telling you, it sounds like some kind of sketchy contract with the mafia or a money-laundering scheme for a drug cartel or something," Gretchen said. "If they sell it every few years, they clearly have a system in place. You don't want to find out what will happen if you get in their way. It's probably why the previous owners were so eager to sell it."

"Yeah, Thia," Deidre agreed, "maybe you should sell Blairmont and start your business somewhere else. How many other places did you have on your list?"

"No," Thia said. "Blairmont is perfect. It's secluded, yet close to the town square. It has plenty of forest for hikes and trails. It has beautiful gardens, a lake, and, most of all, a historic home that is breathtaking. It's too perfect to give up."

"I don't know, Thia," Deidre said. "This is starting to sound scary."

"Yeah," Gretchen agreed, "at the very least, you shouldn't be staying there alone."

"Yeah, stay at my place tonight," Deidre suggested.

"I'll be fine," Thia said, pulling out her phone. "Look." She opened the security app while she continued, "I had cameras installed so I can check to see if anyone is in the house, either when I'm there and think I hear a noise or like now when I'm away."

An error message appeared, saying, "No data available."

"What?" Thia exclaimed. "Hold on."

She closed the app, turned off her phone, turned it back on, and restarted the app.

Again, it read, "No data available."

"Sorry," she told the girls as she stood up. "I have to call them."

She went outside, dialed the number for the security company, and told them about the error. With profuse apologies, they told her there appeared to be some kind of malfunction and that they would send someone out to fix the problem immediately.

When she returned, Thia put cash on the table to pay for her drink and told Deidre and Gretchen she had to leave to meet the security company.

"Let me come with you," Gretchen said.

"No, I'll be fine," Thia assured her.

"But you'll come to my apartment afterward, right?" Deidre asked.

"Maybe," Thia said, seriously considering it. "We'll see how late it is by the time this gets sorted out."

AS SHE DROVE BACK TO BLAIRMONT, THIA FOUND herself viewing that secluded drive differently. The forest on each side, which she had originally thought of as peaceful and relaxing, now felt ominous and scary. Anything—or anyone—could be hiding within those trees.

The road that was but a mile might as well have been ten, a hundred, or even a thousand miles on a night like this one. A light mist had settled on the windshield to disrupt the view just enough to be askew and unclear, giving the familiar stretch an unfamiliar feel, as if the road had changed while she was away. A small portion of the forest along the drive was overrun with kudzu, and as she drove past it, the vine looked as if it could reach out, enwrap her car, and pull her into the woods, never to be found. Driving that mile in the dark, from the comfortable, well-lit, bustling little town square to her disquieting, dim, empty corner of the world, Thia felt like she might as well have been driving through a metaphysical phenomenon, like she was traveling through a portal that took her to a place that was entirely otherworldly.

She remembered Carol offering to show her a house "closer to town," and now she could see how it was that Carol viewed it that way. Though just a mile, the thick forest and winding road made it so the estate was completely separated.

No, not separated. *Isolated.*

As she approached the manor, she was relieved to see a van with the security company logo already parked in her driveway. She looked forward to the day when her business was so busy that she would never drive up to an empty house. Over the next hour, she turned on all the lights, offered refreshments to the person from the security company, and felt more at ease than she had on the drive back, attributing her trepidation on the one-mile stretch to loneliness. So after the cameras were fixed and the system was working properly again, she sent a text to Gretchen and Deidre, letting them know that all was well and that she had decided to stay at Blairmont.

That night, she slept in a new room. She was still working her way through all the bedrooms, staying a night in each one to see for herself that they were ready for guests. As she had done every evening since the girls had stayed for the weekend, Thia made sure all the deadbolts on the servant-access doors were locked, and then she locked all the bedrooms from the outside with her master key. In the room where she stayed, she made sure the servant door was locked. Then, with all her strength, she shoved the large wooden dresser across the floor so it was positioned in front of the disguised door. She turned the deadbolt and secured the swing bar lock on the bedroom door, checked the security cameras on her phone, and turned off the lights.

In the middle of the night, still half-asleep, she got up to use the restroom. She had not turned on any lights when she got up, so when she turned off the bathroom light, the bedroom seemed darker than it had before. Momentarily blind while her eyes readjusted to the dark, she felt the wall for guidance as she walked back to the bed. Approaching the dresser, she reached out to place her hand on it, but instead of the hard wooden surface of the dresser, she felt the soft fleshy palm of a human hand.

She screamed as she jerked her hand back, but the other hand tightened its grip around hers and held on.

Still screaming, she felt with her other hand for the light switch on the wall just inside the bathroom behind her. As the bathroom light came on, the mysterious hand in the dark released its grasp.

There was nobody there.

With shaky breaths, she quickly looked down at her hand and then around the room. The large dresser was still in front of the hidden door, which was shut and locked. The main door to the bedroom was also shut, with both the deadbolt and swing bar locks in place.

She retrieved her phone from the nightstand and checked the footage from the security cameras. They all showed no activity.

She walked to the bedroom door, unlocked it, and slowly opened it, just enough to stick her head out and peek down the corridor.

There was no trace of anyone else having been there.

She held her breath and stayed completely still, listening.

It was silent.

With how creaky the floors were, she felt certain she would have heard the floorboards if someone had been in the room or hallway. And with the door locked, including the swing bar lock that could only be unlatched from the inside, she knew logically that it was impossible for someone to have been in the room with her. Furthermore, looking at the space between the dresser and where she had likely been standing when the incident occurred, there was no room for another human being.

She let out all her breath in complete exhalation, relieved in her assurance that it was impossible for anyone else to have been there. She switched the light off and went back to bed, convinced it had been just a dream, likely induced by her endless paranoid thoughts of some conspiracy by the town council to get her to sell Blairmont so they would get the commission from the sale. It sounded so ludicrous when she thought it through.

Still, the incident made it clear to Thia that the cameras and new locks were not enough for her to have peace of mind. The locks could be picked; the security cameras could go out or be hacked. And although she could not believe someone would actually break into her home, she could not focus on her work if she was constantly worried, even if only in the back of her mind, that someone was in the house. She knew she would not be at ease until all the permits and licenses were approved and the hotel was full of guests and a staff to serve them. Until then, she needed a way to know if someone was in the house without having to constantly watch the video feed from the security cameras.

So the next morning, she sat with her cup of coffee in one of the chairs by the lake and thought of ways she could solve this problem, how she could continue to move forward with getting the business going without having to worry about saboteurs in her house. She considered having an alarm system installed, but she did not plan on keeping it active when the hotel was open. Given that she planned on opening as soon as her permits and licenses were granted, which could be any day now, the benefit did not outweigh the cost. It was then that she remembered the bell collar on Valerie's cat and came up with the ingenious idea to put bells on the door handles.

She pulled up the maps app on her phone and searched for the nearest pet supply store. Seeing that it was already open, she drove there right away to check if they had any of the collars in stock so she could try one out. Next to the ones with a single bell, however, were some with not only one bell but five, evenly spaced all along the collar. They were larger and louder, too. The store was mayhem because the computers were down, so she went to the nearest ATM, pulled out cash, returned to the store, and put all the bell collars they had left in stock in her shopping basket. With angry customers all around and Thia eager to get back home to work on her plan, she calculated the amount it would cost and put enough cash on the counter to cover it, telling the overwhelmed clerk not to worry about giving her change or a handwritten receipt.

She went home and spent the rest of the afternoon using ribbons to wrap the bell collars around the doorknobs on the inside, checking to make sure they were secure and would jingle when the handle was touched from the outside.

Days went by without incident, and Thia was finally able to concentrate on her work again. All was well, and she had no cause for concern.

But then one night, she was awoken by the bells.

At first, when her head was still groggy from waking up from interrupted deep sleep, and because the storm outside was so loud, she was not sure what had woken her. A flash of lightning outside the window lit the room to near daylight, the crashing sound of thunder following almost immediately. She assumed, then, that it must have been the storm that woke her, even though she was known to sleep soundly through the loudest of noises—music, parties, fireworks, sirens—this storm was quiet by comparison. But then, once the sound of thunder had died down, over the sound of heavy rain pelting against the windows, she heard a door shut down the hall. She realized, then, that the bells ringing must have been what had brought her out of slumber, for an unfamiliar sound such as that would wake even the heaviest of sleepers.

She sat up, listening more intently, and she distinctly heard the creaking of floorboards, the shuffling sound of feet walking across carpet, and the unmistakable jingling of bells on a door handle.

She reached for her phone on the nightstand and checked the camera in the hallway. An error message read, "No data available."

Thinking the storm may have interfered with the signal, she checked the other cameras.

They were all, each and every single one, still working.

All the while, she could hear the faint noises in the distance down the hall at the other end of the wing: a door closing, creaking floorboards, the turn of a deadbolt lock, the unmistakable jingling of bells, a squeaky hinge, and then the door shutting. Footsteps on the creaky floorboards as they crossed the hallway. The sharp scraping sound of the deadbolt lock turning. The high-pitched metallic jingling of the bells on the collar on the inside door handle. The squeaky hinges of the door swinging. The final click as the door was closed.

Thia looked at the door to the bedroom she was sleeping in that night, able to see in the darkness that the deadbolt was still locked. But all the rooms were locked. Her only solace was that her door had the additional swing bar lock in place.

The sounds were getting closer, systematically working their way down the hall toward her room: footsteps on creaking floorboards, accompanied by the rhythmic shake of high-pitched metallic bells as the person carrying them took each step; a deadbolt lock turning; the faint jingling of a single bell collar having been disturbed by the rotating doorknob; squeaking hinges as the door swung open and closed; a clicking sound as the door was shut.

Then across the hall from that one: Floorboards. Lock. Bells. Hinges. Door.

Even closer now: Creaking. Turning. Jingling. Squeaking. Click.

Phone in hand, Thia slid out from under the covers, carefully crept across the floor, and crawled into the wardrobe. She silently pulled the door shut and dialed 911.

Immediately, a dispatcher answered. "911, what's your emergency?"

Cupping her hand over her mouth and the mic at the bottom of her phone, Thia whispered as quietly as she could, "There's someone in my house."

7

"WHERE ARE YOU, AND WHERE IS THE INTRUDER?" the dispatcher asked.

"I'm in a bedroom," Thia whispered. "I just got in the wardrobe and shut the door, but I can hear them in the hallway." She gave the dispatcher her name, address, and her exact location in the house. The dispatcher told her the police had been notified and were on their way.

Thia stayed quiet and listened. She could hear the bells of each room as each door was opened and then shut. The faint little chimes were rhythmic, bouncing with each step.

"I can hear them coming," she whispered.

The dispatcher replied, "Okay, stay as quiet as you can and stay as calm as you can. Help is on the way."

Thia heard the bells on the inside doorknob of the bedroom she was in. Then, she heard the door hinges squeak as it swung open. She sat completely still and held her breath, turning the in-call volume of her phone all the way down and saying a prayer in her mind that the dispatcher would stay quiet. She slid her thumb over the speaker on her phone and held the screen to her chest so the light from it would not be seen through the crack under the wardrobe door.

She heard the bells on the door of her bedroom chime again, starting softly and then louder and louder and louder, not only the bells on her door but all the bells now, from all the doors, as if being shaken on purpose, as if the intruder knew she was listening. And then, impossibly, the jangling of all the bells was so loud she could have sworn the intruder was right outside the wardrobe, menacingly shaking the bells, taunting her.

And then silence.

For what felt like an eternity, she waited for any sound, any clue as to where the intruder was at that moment.

She thought of each person from the town, every single one she could remember having an encounter with—a conversation, a greeting, a moment of eye contact. She had suspected nobody here liked her, that at least one person was trying to get rid of her, but for her life she could not think of a single person, specifically, who had given her any indication they would go so far as to break into her home.

The eternal silence continued until she heard the bedroom handle being jiggled and then loud knocking on the door.

Thia screamed and dropped her phone.

"Cynthia Watkins?" she heard someone ask.

Thia yelled, "Yes, I'm here!" as she shoved the doors to the wardrobe open and picked up her phone. She told the dispatcher, "The police are here."

As she walked across the room to the bedroom door, the dispatcher told Thia, "Okay, I'm glad to hear you're safe now."

"Thank you," Thia said, nearly in tears from relief.

"Have a good night, and stay safe," the dispatcher said.

Thia ended the call, unlocked the deadbolt, and

unlatched the swing bar lock. "I'm coming out," she told the police on the other side.

Upon opening the door, she saw two deputies, each with their guns drawn and holding flashlights, facing opposite directions to cover the hallway.

Without looking at her, one of the deputies asked, "Is there anyone else in the room with you?"

The other deputy frantically swiveled to shine his flashlight all around him and down the hallway.

"No," Thia said. "There's no one else in the house."

"Okay, get behind me," the first deputy said. "We'll walk you out first, and then we'll clear the rooms."

Thia stepped out of the room and into the hallway, between the two deputies. As they began to leave, the deputy who had spoken to Thia spoke into her radio to request backup for searching the premises. The deputy behind her quickly looked to each side and then behind him. He continued with that swiveling motion, rotating from facing the direction they were walking, then side to side, and then behind him, all the way down the hall. As they approached a light switch on the wall, Thia reached out to turn on the lights, but none came on.

"The power's out for most of the town," the deputy in front of her said.

The deputy in front of her held her flashlight up at shoulder level, so Thia turned on the flashlight app on her phone and held it so it illuminated the floor directly ahead of them.

"Thanks," the deputy in front of her said.

The rotating light from the deputy behind her caused odd shadows to appear at random as they made their way down the hall, down the stairs, and to the front entrance.

Thia tried to listen for any sounds of the intruder, but she could hardly hear anything over the storm outside and the sounds of her own anxious, shaky breathing.

Once outside, they had to yell over the torrential downpour, the heavy drops falling in a straight line from the sky to the ground.

"We'll wait in the car until backup arrives," the deputy shouted, pointing at the SUV parked at the foot of the stairs.

They ran to it, their clothes becoming drenched in the few seconds it took for them to get from the covered veranda to the inside of the vehicle. Thia quickly got into the back seat, while the deputy who had walked behind her got into the front passenger side, and the deputy who had walked in front of her ran around the front of the vehicle to get into the driver's seat. Once inside, she started the engine and turned on the heat to help them dry off.

The rain was louder in the car, beating down on the roof.

Turning around to face Thia, the deputy in the driver's seat yelled, "I'm Deputy Lawrence." Then, she pointed at the deputy in the passenger seat and yelled, "And this is Deputy Carver. I didn't see any sign of a break-in, but we'll check and make sure it's empty before you go back inside."

"Let's wait in town," Deputy Carver shouted.

Deputy Lawrence rolled her eyes and continued, "Usually, once the cops show up, the suspects flee, so whoever was in there is probably gone now. But when we get calls like this, we clear the premises before allowing anyone to go back inside. I called for backup because I'm not sure we can confirm it's empty with only the two of us. There are too many wings and staircases. You may want to prepare yourself for the possibility that we won't be able to assure you that it's empty. Do you have any kind of alarm system or security cameras you could check?"

"Yes, I have security cameras," Thia shouted, pulling up the security app on her phone.

Continuing to swivel so he could check the surrounding area, Deputy Carver shouted, "Let's get out of here. She shouldn't go back inside anyway."

"Why not?" Thia asked.

Ignoring him, Deputy Lawrence asked Thia, "Are you able to access the cameras?"

"There's no signal," Thia shouted, "probably due to the power outage. But before the power went out, I checked them, and all the cameras were working, except the one that covered the hallway where I was sleeping. So I think whoever did this somehow turned off the camera so they wouldn't be seen. I'll see if I can figure out how to access the recorded footage from the other cameras."

Deputy Carver made a noise and Thia thought she heard him mumble, "We shouldn't be here."

She searched the recorded footage from the security cameras, starting with the one positioned at the gatekeeper's house and then the ones that covered the external doors of the main house. Meanwhile, Deputy Carver continued to shift and squirm in his seat as he continually looked out all the windows of the car. With the power outage, there were no outdoor lights, and the downpour made it so there was little visibility, even with the headlights on.

After nearly ten minutes in the car, they saw headlights approaching. Deputy Lawrence got out of the car and met with the four additional deputies who had arrived, the five of them discussing their strategy on the veranda before going in.

"I thought Daffodil had its own police department," Thia

shouted to Deputy Carver, who she assumed was still in the car as a protective measure for her. "Why didn't they respond to the call?"

"They don't come out here," he shouted, still continually checking the surrounding area as much as he could.

"But Blairmont is well within the city limits," Thia argued, suspicion rising in her mind as she recalled Deidre and Gretchen suggesting corruption and organized crime.

"They just don't," he snapped. "Neither should we. No one should be out here."

They sat in silence, both unnerved and anxious, though Thia did not know why Deputy Carver was so afraid. For her, it was obvious: someone had broken into her home. But not knowing why he was so unhinged, wondering what he knew that she did not, only made her more worried. She began to imagine all the possible reasons as to why he thought they should not be there. She imagined what could have happened to her if they had not come—and what kind of powerful figure must have been behind this if the Daffodil Police Department would not get involved.

Finally, the five deputies emerged from the front doors. When Deputy Lawrence got back into the driver's seat, she said, "It's clear, but we couldn't do a thorough check of the outside. We'll send someone back in the morning to be sure. It will be easier to find small pieces of evidence they may have left behind once the sun is up and the weather has cleared. In the meantime, you should stay somewhere else tonight, just in case."

"It's two o'clock in the morning," Thia said.

"Do you have a friend or family member you can call?"

"Yes, I can go to my mom's house," Thia said, "but my keys and my purse are inside."

"We'll go back and get them with you." Deputy Lawrence got out, and when Deputy Carver did not, she motioned with her hand for him to get out, too. Deputy Lawrence opened the back door for Thia, and the three of them went inside.

"Is it okay if I change clothes?" Thia asked.

At the same time, Deputy Carver said, "No," while Deputy Lawrence said, "Yes."

"Do you want us to come with you?" Deputy Lawrence asked.

Deputy Carver continued to wave the flashlight around as quickly as he could, trying to shine light on as much of the entrance hall as possible.

Thia looked at Deputy Lawrence and then at Deputy Carver, unsure of what to do. On the one hand, Deputy Lawrence had just cleared the house and seemed confident in their ability to protect her. On the other hand, Deputy Carver seemed like he knew more about what was really going on and what real danger was present. In the end, his fear won out over Deputy Lawrence's confidence.

"I'll just get my keys and my purse," Thia said. "They're over here." She picked them up from the table in the entrance hall.

As Thia began to lock the front doors, Deputy Carver ran down the stairs and got into their vehicle. Still shaken by the events of the evening, and even more so by her recurring thoughts of all the possible reasons why Deputy Carver was so jumpy, Thia missed the keyhole several times before dropping her keys.

Deputy Lawrence picked them up and said, "How about I drive? I don't think you're in any shape to get behind the wheel, especially in this weather. Carver can follow us."

But when she told him the plan, he said, "I'm not driving out of here alone."

"Really?" Deputy Lawrence asked. Seeing that he was adamant about this, she rolled her eyes and asked Thia, "Would your mom be able to drive you back tomorrow morning to meet with the investigator?"

"Yes," Thia said.

Deputy Lawrence opened the passenger door and told her partner to get in the back, saying, "Scaredy-cats don't get to ride shotgun."

He did not seem to care, just relieved to be leaving. Thia quickly moved out of his way as he jumped out of the front seat to get into the back.

Deputy Lawrence walked around the front of the car, leaving the front passenger door open.

"Are you sure?" Thia shouted. "I don't mind riding in the back."

"Get in," Deputy Lawrence said, so Thia did.

As they drove off, Deputy Lawrence told Thia, "He's been obnoxious about this from the moment we got the call, so he deserves it." Then, turning to look at him in the back, she said, "And he knows it."

"Can't we just get out of here?" he asked. "Go faster."

"Not in this weather," she responded. The conditions had become worse, the rain so heavy now it sounded like thick hail pounding on the roof, hood, and windows of the vehicle. Deputy Lawrence had the windshield wipers going as fast as they could go, but they did little to clear the view. Thia could barely see in front of her.

Deputy Lawrence continued to drive cautiously, her hands gripping the steering wheel, carefully checking the area around them as she tried to anticipate the next curve in the driveway. As they passed the gatekeeper's house and got on the secluded road, Deputy Carver huffed and sat back in the seat, seeming to finally relax. Deputy Lawrence shook her head, clearly still upset with him. Thia uncomfortably looked straight ahead, feeling as though this would be a long ride if the two deputies were going to act this way the entire time.

After a long minute of silence, Thia felt the tip of a bony finger press on her left shoulder two times. She turned around to look at Deputy Carver and asked, "Yes?"

"Yes what?" he asked.

"Didn't you just tap me on the shoulder?"

"*What?* No!" he exclaimed. He looked next to him in the back seat and scooted himself as close to the door as possible. "Is she in here? Did you bring her with you?"

"Who?" Thia asked, while Deputy Lawrence said, "There's no one else in here."

Panicking, he tried to open the door or roll down the window. "Stop the car!" he commanded. "Let me out!"

"Stop freaking out."

"Sheila, let me out right now!"

Deputy Lawrence stopped the vehicle, put it in park, got out, and opened the door for him. As soon as the door was open, he practically fell out of the back seat and onto the road, so eager was he to get out.

"We're surrounded by woods," Deputy Lawrence shouted. "There could be bears, a burglar..."

"I have my gun," he said. "I can handle anything out here. I can't protect myself from whatever she brought with her."

"I can't just leave you out here like this."

As Thia watched, she thought she heard faint, low, hollow laughter behind her. She turned in the direction of the sound. The back seat was empty, but she could not see the trunk.

"I'm not getting back in there," he said, wiping rainwater from his eyes.

With sheets of rain falling on them, their uniforms were soaked through.

"I can ride in the back," Thia yelled to them.

"I'm not getting back in that vehicle at all." He pulled his phone out of his pocket and said, "I'm calling for a ride right now. Just go without me."

Clearly irritated, Deputy Lawrence slammed the back door shut and returned to the driver's seat. "Good luck," she told him before shutting her door and driving off.

"Is he going to be okay?" Thia asked, turning around to see him through the back window. He was running in their direction, away from Blairmont, phone held up to his ear.

"Don't mind him," Deputy Lawrence said. "He's just a dumb hillbilly, scared of a stupid myth."

They spent the remainder of the car ride in silence. Thia did not ask Deputy Lawrence what the myth was that she was referring to, but Thia was certain the town council—or whoever was trying to run her out of town—was behind it.

THE NEXT MORNING, THIA'S MOTHER DROVE HER back to Blairmont Manor, telling her repeatedly how unsafe she thought it was and that she wanted Thia to move in with her until the hotel was full of guests and staff members—and maybe even then to still live with her.

"It's not safe," she kept saying. "That man warned us, and he was right."

"It's just someone trying to scare me," Thia said.

"Well, they're scaring me," her mother said.

It was the longest car ride of her life, and she eventually stared out the window as her mother went on and on, lecturing her about what she should do.

At the house, the sheriff and a team of deputies were already searching the outside, examining all the windows and doors, searching for signs of tampering with locks or handles. Thia let them inside, and they searched for signs of an intruder.

They found none.

The deputies walked through the house with Thia as she led them from room to room, her mother following behind them, seeing if anything was missing or out of place. In addition to Thia's personal memory, she had pictures of each room that she had taken for the insurance company. While the deputies compared what they saw before them in the house to the pictures she had given them, Thia searched the rooms, including drawers and cabinets, for any evidence that the intruder had been there.

They searched for hours and found nothing: no disturbance in the grass around the doors or windows, no tampering with locks or handles, no broken windows, no missing objects.

"Doesn't look like they took anything," the sheriff said when they were finished.

"Except for the bells," Thia said.

"The bells?" the sheriff asked.

"I had put bell collars on all the bedroom doors and some other doors in the house, too. I put them there so I would hear if anyone was in the house without having to check the security cameras or in case the cameras went out, which one did." She pulled out her phone and showed him the footage from the one that covered the third floor hallway in the wing where she had been sleeping. "See," she said when the screen suddenly went black. "I think someone hacked into the security system so they wouldn't be seen."

"Have you reported it with the company?" the sheriff asked.

"Not yet," Thia replied.

The sheriff was silent for a moment, thinking. Finally, he said, "Bells?"

"Yes," Thia said. "Collars, actually, like for a cat, but they had little bells on them. I secured them with ribbons to the inside door handles and tested them myself. They would make noise when the doorknob was turned, even if very slowly."

"And you had them on the door of your bedroom, too?"

"Yes, but I heard them all down the hallway. That's why I called 911. And all the doors were locked, so whoever did this had a key. I checked the safe, and all the keys to the rooms are still in there. And the master key is on my keychain."

"Does anyone else have access to the keys?" the sheriff asked, making a note.

"The guy who installed the locks, I guess," Thia said, "but I really don't think it was him."

She gave the sheriff his name and phone number anyway, so they could rule him out as a suspect.

"It's kind of odd that with a house full of so many valuable items, the intruder would only take cheap bell collars, don't you think?" the sheriff asked.

"I don't think robbery was the motive here," Thia said. She told him about her suspicion that the town council was trying to run her out so they could get the commission from the sale, as it was the deal they seemed to have with Carol, the realtor who sold her the property.

Being the first time she heard of this, Thia's mother gasped and asked, "Thia, how long have you known about this?"

Ignoring her mother, Thia continued, "Whoever did this was taking the bells on purpose, as a sign. They even stayed at my door and rang them loudly when they couldn't get in because I had the swing bar lock in place. You can ask the 911 dispatcher. I'm sure she heard them, too."

After making some more notes, he said, "Can you think of anyone in particular who might have done this?"

Thia shrugged and said, "No, not specifically."

"All right, then," he said, looking at his notes in his notepad. "I'll speak with Millie, Herschel, Carol, this handyman, and the town council. But I have to be straight with you," he added, closing his notepad, "with no evidence found here, and with only some bells missing, it's highly unlikely we're going to find the culprit. But I'll file a report so it's at least on record."

"That's it?" Thia's mother asked.

"If this is a pattern, whoever did this might do it to someone else, and if they get caught, we'll be able to link them back to this crime, too." In an apologetic tone, he added, "It's the best I can offer with what we have to work with right now."

"I understand," Thia said. "Thank you for coming out here and checking."

"Of course," he said before leaving with his team.

"Thia, I don't like this one bit," her mother said after they left.

"It will be fine." Thia sat down in the nearest chair. "It's just someone trying to bully me. But this is my house, and I have the law on my side. And it's probably only one cowardly person. All they've done is show me they can get inside my house."

"So far," her mother said, sitting next to her. "It's a warning, Thia. They're letting you know they can get to you and that the cops can't do anything about it. Next, they'll do something *to* you. I want you to move in with me. You can't live here."

"This is my home," Thia said with certitude. "If I leave, they win. I'm not going to let them think they can scare me."

"Then I'm staying here, too," her mother declared. "You can't stay here alone."

"Fine," Thia said, too exhausted to argue any further.

She called the security company to tell them about the camera. They agreed that it did go out, but they could find no evidence it had been hacked or tampered with in any way. They made a note of it, but other than that, they said there was nothing they could do, aside from replacing the camera. Thia told them that yes, she did want them to replace it, in case this one was defective, and they scheduled a time for the camera to be replaced.

The sheriff called several hours later to tell her that neither Carol, Millie, Herschel, nor any members of the town council knew anything about the break-in. The handyman promised he did not keep any copies of any keys, and the sheriff had no reason to believe he was lying. Millie did not remember ever seeing any bells at all. And the 911 dispatcher had not heard any bells while on the call with Thia, nor could the sheriff hear any when he listened to the recording of the 911 call himself.

With a sigh, Thia thanked him for all the work he had done and ended the call. Feeling totally discouraged, she tried to remember being in the wardrobe on the phone with the 911 dispatcher when she heard the bells. She remembered clearly that she had put one finger over the speaker to muffle any sound in case the 911 dispatcher said anything. She also remembered holding the phone to her chest so no light could be seen from the screen. But maybe by doing that she had also inadvertently covered the microphone so the bells could not be heard.

She tried to remember if the bells had been on the door handle after she ended the 911 call. But with all the commotion, she could not remember hearing, seeing, or feeling them when she opened the door for the deputies. Perhaps they had been there and the intruder removed them after she left with the deputies.

And it was possible Millie had not seen the bells. Blairmont Manor was so big that Millie cleaned it in shifts, so maybe she had only been in rooms that did not have doors since Thia had bought the bells.

And she remembered how hectic the store had been that day and knew that was why she had no receipt to prove, if only to herself, that she had in fact purchased them.

Or maybe, she now found herself considering, there had never been any bells at all.

8

AFTER FOUR UNEVENTFUL DAYS, THIA WAS ABLE TO convince her mother to return to her own house so Thia could resume her work. She had chefs to interview, job postings to list for housekeeping staff and yard crews, financial statements to review, permit and license statuses to check on, marketing and advertising resources to research, contracts with vendors to review with her lawyer, and she had scheduled a forest expert to come out and look at her land to help her design trails—for which she would also need to hire a crew to create and maintain.

Sitting at the kitchen table that afternoon, her mother having left hours earlier, Thia reviewed the notes in her notebook. As she was flipping through the pages, a note, written within other notes, caught her eye. In her own handwriting, it read, *"Give up, little girl. You don't have what it takes."*

What? Thia thought. *Did* I *write this?*

Confused, she continued to stare at the words, trying to remember when the surrounding notes had been made. She turned to previous pages to search for clues. Finding none, she turned to later pages, but she could not recall when or how this note was made. She never would have written it herself; giving up had never crossed her mind. She had always believed she could do this. This was her dream. And she would never refer to herself as "little girl."

Eyes still on the notebook, she reached for her tea, only to feel the empty air. She looked at where her mug was supposed to be, on the table next to her notebook, but there was nothing there. Then, she looked around the rest of the kitchen—on the table, on the countertops, any surface where she might have set it down. It was nowhere to be found. In her memory, she could see the light pink mug she had been drinking out of, with yellow, green, and blue stripes on it, the tea bag in the water, the string with the little tag hanging over the side, the intense taste of cinnamon and orange still on her tongue.

She felt the kettle on the stovetop. It was still warm, giving her an ounce of relief in the assurance that there had at least been the intention of tea at some point recently. Then, she opened the cupboard, and there it was: her light pink mug with yellow, green, and blue stripes on it. And when she picked it up and held it in her hands, it was cold, unused.

And then there was that low, hollow laughter again, the same chuckling she had heard before. She turned in the direction of the sound, but the kitchen was empty.

Had she only thought of making tea but got distracted after turning off the burner? Had she written that note in her notebook?

She thought about the girls' weekend and the past few days when her mother had been staying with her. All the furniture they had moved remained where they had put it. The only echoes were heard in that one hallway—and they were real echoes, being heard from sound waves bouncing off the walls and ceiling, not the solid characteristic of a new sound being generated on the floor nearby. The new linens remained on the beds. Each creak of a floorboard could be attributed to an actual person walking on it. Every sound could be traced back to a precise source. There were never any unaccounted-for shadows that looked like someone else might be in the room, no odd peripheral reflections in the windows or glass furnishings that made it look like someone was standing behind her.

All the odd events in her memory had only happened when she was alone, as this odd event was happening now, while she was alone.

Stress can have a profound effect on the mind, and when the mind is forced to make sense of what one believes to be impossible, the result can sometimes be a view of the world that is inconsistent with true reality. So when Thia thought about all the things on her to-do list and these little lapses in memory and perception she seemed to be having, she considered that maybe Ruth was right. Maybe she was taking on too much at once. The idea that someone was trying to scare her so she would sell Blairmont so the town would get the commission from the sale was already far-fetched. But then to add to it the method of scaring her, by moving things around, closing the gate when she left it open, making her think someone was in the house when she thought she was alone, even though *two* separate teams of deputies were unable to find any evidence—together this was becoming highly improbable, a conspiracy created out of desperation. She was smart, she knew that, and when she thought through everything logically, what actually made the most sense was that this was all in her head.

She pulled out her phone and sent a text to Ruth, asking her about the psychiatrist she had recommended.

ASIDE FROM THE IMPULSIVE ACT OF BUYING A lottery ticket, going to a psychiatrist was, Thia felt, the best decision she had ever made. The session was immensely helpful. To have a professional with whom to talk through everything, to have someone believe her with sympathy and, most importantly, to have a plan of action to help her get through this period of her life, was more than Thia had ever hoped for. The psychiatrist told Thia her symptoms were indeed caused by stress and that they were very mild. She was optimistic that as more things fell into place for the business and as there were less items still up in the air to juggle, Thia would no longer have these hallucinations or paranoid thoughts. She told Thia she did not need medication, that therapy sessions would likely be enough, but Thia wanted to take a more aggressive approach to treating whatever this was that was happening in her mind. So her psychiatrist called in a prescription for her, to be picked up at the pharmacy in the Daffodil town square, and Thia received an alert on her phone that it had already been filled while she was driving back from the city.

When she approached the counter to pick up her medication, however, the pharmacist was not so accommodating.

"Is this where you live?" the pharmacist asked, turning the computer screen toward her so she could see the address they had on file for her.

"Yes," Thia told him, thinking the better way to ensure

she was the patient would have been to ask her to say the address without seeing it first. But little acts of trust like this one only added to Daffodil's small-town charm in Thia's opinion.

"One of the reasons this drug is prescribed is for hallucinations," he said.

"Yes," Thia said, giving half a glance to see if anyone was within eavesdropping distance. As endearing as the small-town attitude was, it meant that everyone knew everyone—and their business. She would have appreciated a little bit more professional discretion.

"When did you start having hallucinations?" he asked.

Okay, small-town charm or not, now he had crossed a line.

"How much will it be?" Thia asked, pulling her billfold out of her purse.

"What have you been seeing?" he asked. "Reflections in the curio? A shadow of someone standing next to a grandfather clock? An extra figure next to one of the lifelike marble statues? Maybe you moved those three chairs along the wall in the front sitting room, only to find them back where they originally were the next time you went in there?"

"I'm sorry," Thia said, "but this is really none of your business."

"I'm going to hold on to this until I hear a second opinion," he said.

"Excuse me?" Thia asked.

"I just don't feel comfortable giving this medication to someone who isn't hallucinating."

Insulted, Thia opened her mouth to protest, but he continued before she had a chance to speak.

"How many locals have you talked to about Blairmont

since you moved here? Or, rather, I guess the better question is how many locals have been willing to talk to you since you moved to Blairmont?"

Thia put her billfold back into her purse and turned to leave.

"Just a second," he said, calling after her as he picked up the phone.

Thia turned back to the counter, willing to hear him out.

He spoke with someone on the phone, something about having enough time to squeeze someone in for an emergency session. "Fifteen minutes is all you'll need," she heard him say.

When he hung up the phone, he pointed toward the front of the store, where there were clear glass windows, and asked, "See that building across the street?"

"Yes," Thia said.

"Dr. Bachmann's office is in the one behind it. It's in an old house that has been converted into office space. His office is on the first floor, first door to the right when you walk in. He can see you in about ten minutes. If he agrees to the script, I'll fill it."

Not believing this situation she was in, but having no choice unless she wanted to get the prescription filled somewhere else, which would require driving back to the city, Thia left the pharmacy to see this "Dr. Bachmann," whoever that was.

She found the old house, and, as the pharmacist had told her, the first door on the right had a sign on it that read, "Dr. Bachmann's office. Please enter quietly."

She slowly opened the door to a small waiting room with chairs, a side table, some magazines, a water cooler with a paper cone dispenser attached to it, and another door on the adjacent wall. Not knowing what else to do, Thia sat in one of the chairs, and after about ten seconds stood up to leave, when the other door opened.

"Ms. Watkins?" a man asked.

"Yes," Thia said.

"Hi, I'm Dr. Bachmann. Come on in." He stepped aside and held his hand out toward his office.

As Thia walked toward him, he asked, "How can I help you?"

"How much is this going to cost?" Thia asked, going past him into the room.

Shutting the door behind him and walking to a chair, he said, "It depends on why you're here and if you have insurance. Dr. Sherman didn't give me much information."

"In the few minutes it took me to walk over here and sit in the waiting room, it occurred to me that you probably have a nice little scam going on here, whereby he refers psychotic patients to you and forces them to go by holding their meds ransom. Then, you represcribe whatever the medication is, and the pharmacist gets a kickback."

"That would be a clever scam indeed," Dr. Bachmann said, sitting in a black leather chair and picking up a notepad and pen. As he made a note, he asked, "Do you have these thoughts often?"

"What thoughts?" Thia asked, still standing by the door.

"That the world is constantly trying to scam you, that the people you come in contact with, supposed strangers, may be plotting your demise?"

"No, of course not, that would be absurd," Thia replied defensively.

"I'm sorry," Dr. Bachmann said in a calming voice. "What can I help you with, then?"

Annoyed, Thia said, "The pharmacist wouldn't give me my prescription until you approved it."

"Okay," Dr. Bachmann said. "Please, have a seat while I figure this out."

Thia chose not to sit while Dr. Bachmann called the pharmacist.

"Hi, Hank, I have Ms. Watkins here, but we're both unclear about why you sent her to me."

Thia watched Dr. Bachmann as he listened to the pharmacist on the other end of the line, his face and tone remaining expressionless.

"I see," he finally said. "All right, I'll let you know."

After he hung up, he turned his attention to Thia and said, "You're the latest resident of Blairmont."

"Yes," Thia confirmed.

"They're not hallucinations."

"I beg your pardon?" Thia asked, annoyed at his assurance of what was going on in her mind.

"Have you talked with other people about Blairmont? The housekeeper? The groundskeeper?"

"No, nobody will talk to me," Thia said, finally sitting down on the couch and setting her purse next to her, realizing that this psychiatrist, this Dr. Bachmann, might finally be a local townsperson who would give her some answers. She continued, "And they all look at me like I'm temporary. Everybody here does, not just Millie and Herschel—Millie and Herschel are the housekeeper and groundskeeper you asked about. I know Blairmont Manor has had many owners, mainly people who only spent weekends or a month in the summer here, but I love the house, and I plan to stay in it. I've really tried to establish myself as a member of this community, but everyone acts like I won't be here long enough for it to be worth their effort to get to know me."

"And this is what bothers you so much?" Dr. Bachmann asked. "Why you went to a psychiatrist to get the prescription for hallucinations?"

"Not only hallucinations," Thia said, relaxing. "Thoughts of paranoia, too, like someone is trying to get me to leave. You see, my life has been turned completely upside down in the last few months, and I think I rushed into everything too quickly. I won the lottery and bought this house and moved away from all my friends. I've always lived in the city, my whole life, and then I moved to a small town, where I didn't know a single soul. I quit my job so I could convert Blairmont Manor into a luxury boutique hotel and run it myself, which has been my dream job since I was a child. And I think it was too much. I should have eased into it more, kept my job at least and maybe my apartment in the city. I should have come only a few days a week at first and then slowly moved out here."

Dr. Bachmann nodded slowly as he listened, his hands resting on the notepad, without taking any notes.

"But I think it was just too much for my brain," Thia continued. "I think I've had a psychotic break of sorts. I'll do something in one room, like rearrange the furniture, and when I go back into the room, it will be the way it was originally. And I can't honestly remember if I actually moved anything or if I only thought about it. I've had to start leaving myself little reminders and notes around the house, like one I wrote yesterday telling me I actually did load the dishwasher—"

At this, he interrupted her and asked, "Approximately how many of those notes would you say you remember writing but then later couldn't find?"

"Maybe half…" Thia said, astounded that this was so common a symptom that he was able to guess it. "Do you think I have early-onset dementia?"

"No," he said. "Tell me about the hallucinations."

"Sometimes I think I see someone, either in a dark room or in a reflection. For example, one night, out of the corner of my eye, I thought I saw something. So I looked at the window, and in the reflection, it looked like there was someone standing behind me. But when I turned around, there was no one there. Or sometimes when I turn off the light to a room, it will look like there's someone standing in it, but then when I turn the light back on, there's no one there."

With typical psychiatrist demeanor, Dr. Bachmann maintained eye contact with Thia and, aside from the occasional nod of encouragement for her to continue, listened attentively without expression. She told him about hearing floorboards creaking and footsteps in the room, as well as low, hollow laughter. She told him about the note in her notebook and the mug being cold when she remembered pouring hot water into it for tea. She told him about hearing the voice whisper in her ear, about feeling the hand in the darkness, about the bells ringing in the night, right outside the wardrobe, where no one would have been able to stand because both the main door and the hidden door to the bedroom were locked.

Once she had finished, Dr. Bachmann remained expressionless as he asked, "Do you see anyone here in the room with us right now?"

Thia gave him a look of annoyance.

"I know that's cliché for a psychiatrist to ask a patient,

but I'm serious. Is she here?"

"She?" Thia asked. "Who? I never said it was a woman."

"Listen," he said, setting his notepad and pen on the desk next to him. "I don't think you're hallucinating, nor do I think you have a form of dementia."

"Then how could I possibly have these thoughts and see these things?" Thia asked.

"I think you've been seeing the ghost."

After a moment of stunned silence, Thia said, "I think I just had another hallucination because it sounded like you said this was all caused by a ghost."

"That's exactly what I said. You're not hallucinating."

Thia's shock was broken by a quick outburst of exhalation, and then she laughed as she asked, "What?"

Dr. Bachmann did not respond, so Thia continued. *"I'm* the patient, and *you're* the psychiatrist, but *you're* the one telling me my symptoms are not psychotic at all but can instead be explained by my house being *haunted?"* Now, after saying it out loud, she was laughing. "And this is why Dr. Sherman wouldn't fill the order? Because he thinks my house is haunted, too?"

"Yes," Dr. Bachmann said in all seriousness. "In fact, the whole town does."

Thia laughed again and said, "Wow," as she put her purse over her shoulder and stood up. "I'm not paying for this," she told him. "I have half a mind to report you both."

"Ms. Watkins," Dr. Bachmann said, standing up, too.

"No," Thia said. "I'm getting my prescription filled in the city."

"I'll tell him to fill it," Dr. Bachmann said, getting Thia's attention. "Dr. Sherman told me what your psychiatrist prescribed for you, and it's a very low dose, so low I'm not sure it would have an effect beyond a placebo anyway. But take the meds and see for yourself. If they work and all this goes away, I'll be the first to admit I'm a quack. But if you think they're not working—seriously, at the first instance that you think you're hallucinating or thought you did something but now you're not sure—call this number." He wrote down a number on the notepad, tore out the sheet, and handed it to her. "It's my work mobile phone, so you can call it anytime."

"But you will call Dr. Sherman to tell him to give me my meds?" Thia confirmed.

"You can watch me do it right now."

Dr. Bachmann made the call, and Thia waited until it was done.

"Thank you," she said and headed toward the door.

"Actually, the exit is this way." Dr. Bachmann held his hand out toward a door that led outside. "It helps to maintain privacy in case my next patient is in the waiting room."

She left Dr. Bachmann's office, resisting the temptation to rip up the piece of paper with his work cell phone number on it, and tried not to act too smug when Dr. Sherman gave her the medication her actual psychiatrist had prescribed for her.

In her kitchen at home, she took a pen and vigorously scribbled over the note she did not remember writing in her notebook. Then, with a huff, she filled a glass with water and swallowed the pill before getting back to work.

9

FOR AN ENTIRE WEEK, THIA WORKED WITHOUT disruption or distraction. Since moving to Blairmont Manor, she had researched vendors and companies she could work with, and she had even begun negotiations, but there were always too many interruptions for her to make concrete decisions or sign any contracts. In this one week, however, she got more plans finalized than she had during her entire residency at Blairmont thus far.

All her permits and licenses were approved. An official viewed the estate, and it was currently pending approval for the registry of historic places. She met with the forester to design trails and hired a company to make them. She found a housekeeping company that would send employees to her hotel when she needed them, until her business was busy enough for her to hire her own staff.

She was able to negotiate a price with a winery two hours away so she could offer a complimentary bottle with each room, serve their wines in the dining hall, and sell their wines at the gift shop. She worked with high-end companies to negotiate similar deals for hair and skin products and specialty soaps that she would provide in bathrooms and sell at the gift shop. And with all of these vendors, she signed one-year contracts, confident she would be able to renegotiate and get better deals once she showed them her business was successful.

Everything was finally coming together. She wished she could have had it all done in time to throw a Halloween party—now just two days away—or have a fall festival, where she would invite the entire town. But she was happy with the way things were coming along. Being less than a month away, a Thanksgiving event was probably out of the question, too, but she was already putting together Christmas decorations and was hoping to host a party at that time.

She had taken over the original office as her own and was finishing up after a long day. She checked a few more items in her notes to make sure she had everything ready for the following day, and when she was satisfied that she was at a stopping point, she closed her notebook with a smile. Checking her phone, she saw that it was nearly nine o'clock, and she still had not yet eaten dinner. She left her work at her desk and headed for the kitchen. On her way out, she switched off the light, and the figure of a person appeared standing next to her desk.

Stumbling backward as she gasped, Thia felt for the light switch on the wall and turned the light back on.

The room was empty.

It's not real, she told herself. *It's not real.*

She had been warned by her psychiatrist to make sure she ate properly, got enough sleep, and took care not to push herself too much. This hallucination was just a symptom, she told herself, just a reminder that she had to stay on top of her health.

She switched the light off and checked the room again.

It was empty.

After eating, she went straight to bed, determined to keep her symptoms under control with a healthy lifestyle in addition to her medication. With everything coming together, however, and with the hotel soon to have its soft opening right before the holidays, she was as optimistic as her psychiatrist that her mind would settle down once everything *actually* started happening, once guests and customers *actually* started arriving. For now, it was only one hallucination. It was no cause for concern.

But then, that night, while she was sleeping, she had a dream she was down at the lake. In her dream, she put her hand in the icy cold water, and the sensation was as real to her as if she had been wide awake and fully alert. Suddenly, her eyes shot open as she realized it was not a dream—or rather, not fully. She sat up and looked around herself. She was still in bed, but her hand was freezing…and wet. Drenched, really. She smelled her hand, and it even *smelled* like lake water. On the floor next to her bed, beneath where her hand had been hanging over the edge, was a puddle, and leading away from her bed were drops of water.

She got up and followed the drops from the bedroom where she was sleeping, down the hall, down the stairs, and to one of the back doors that led outside.

Thia stood, staring at the drops of water on the marble floor of the back entrance hall, stunned. She had never sleepwalked before. Then, coming to her senses, she went to the nearest bathroom and got a hand towel to wipe up the water. Starting at that one back door where she had apparently come in from outside, she followed the trail of water drops, drying marble, hardwood, and carpet, all the way back to the room in which she had been sleeping. She sat on the bed a moment, phone in hand, going back and forth in her mind as to whether or not she should call the number Dr. Bachmann had given her.

I should go back to sleep, she thought, knowing rest was ultimately what she needed.

But she was too alert and on edge to do that. What if she sleepwalked again? What if she fell into the lake and drowned?

Deciding a cup of herbal tea would help calm her down and perhaps help her sleep again, Thia slipped on her house shoes, put on a robe over her pajamas, and went to the kitchen, phone still in hand. As she waited for the water to boil, she decided she did not need to call Dr. Bachmann tonight. Thus far, she had seen only one hallucination and had sleepwalked. There was a chance she would have no more symptoms if she took better care of her health in the future. On her phone, she set alarms to remind herself to eat, and that already put her mind at ease.

Once the tea was ready, she put her phone in the pocket of her robe and went to the front of the house to sit in her favorite sitting room. She sat in an antique velvet chair, the cushion feeling as if she were the first person to ever sit in it, and cupped the warm mug with both of her hands. She did not want to sleep for fear of sleepwalking again. Apparently, even asleep she remembered to unlock the deadbolt and unlatch the swing bar lock. What if next time she moved the furniture from in front of the hidden door and got lost in the servants' hallways?

As she contemplated these thoughts, she became aware of the curtain in front of her moving, just barely, just ever so slightly, so slowly that in her unsteady state of mind she could easily convince herself it was not actually moving at all, that it was just an illusion. It was a thick curtain, this being one of the sitting rooms at the front of the house, the one immediately to the right of the front hall with the grand staircase and those two huge, heavy wooden doors. The ceiling in this room was high, the windows nearly two stories, the curtains long and heavy to cover them. But, yes, as she stared straight ahead, she could see that the curtain was slowly, slowly, *slowly* shifting in an unnatural way, almost as if it were coming toward her, little by little, bit by bit.

After nearly fifteen minutes of being mesmerized by the incredibly *slow* but fluid movement, a blink of her eyes allowed Thia to perceive what had taken form before her: a face outlined in the cloth and the appearance of a person, as if someone were standing between the curtain and the window, stretching the fabric so it conformed to the shape of a human body.

With a loud, high-pitched scream, she jumped up from the chair, her mug of tea flying in the air and crashing to the floor as she tried to get away. She turned to run but immediately tripped and fell to the floor, catching herself with her hands. She turned on her back and looked at the curtain. It was long, still, and in place, hanging directly in front of the window without the slightest swaying, as if it had not been disturbed at all.

She reached into her robe pocket and pulled out her phone. Her symptoms were returning in full force. She ran to the office and found the sheet of paper Dr. Bachmann had given her and dialed the number as she walked back to the sitting room, stepping into a hallway bathroom on the way for a towel so she could clean up her mess.

After three rings, he answered.

"Hello, Dr. Bachmann?" Thia said, crouching down to wipe up the spilt tea. She would need to have the antique rug professionally cleaned, but luckily it was a dark rug, so the stain was barely noticeable for now. Still, she made a mental note to either talk with the housekeeping company she had hired or find a company that specialized in antiques to do the job.

"Yes?" he said. "Who's calling?"

"It's Thia Watkins," she said. "I'm so sorry to bother you at this hour, but I can't go back to sleep for fear of sleepwalking. But I also can't stay awake because my hallucinations are back, and I don't know what I should do."

"Do you have a habit of sleepwalking?"

"No, but I did tonight, apparently, and now I've made a mess because I thought I saw something—"

"Get out of the house," he warned with urgency, not at all like the expressionless professional he had been when they first met. "Now!"

"What?" Thia asked, thinking she must not have heard him correctly. "I'm in my night clothes."

"It doesn't matter," he said, sounding frantic now.

"I guess I could get dressed, but where would I go?"

"Don't get dressed. Don't get your keys or your purse or anything else. Just make it obvious you are leaving. Get out of the house right now and start running toward the town square. I'm on my way. I'll find you and pick you up."

"What?" she asked again, not believing what she was hearing. "You can't be serious."

Just then, she was lifted up to her feet, turned so she was facing the door, and shoved forward by an unseen force.

Stumbling in an effort to be in control of her own movements, she tried to turn her head around to see what was happening, to see *who* was behind her, forcing her out of the house.

In a state of total confusion, if not shock, Thia was vaguely aware of her senses: The sounds through the phone of Dr. Bachmann getting into his car—the jingling of keys, the thud of a door slamming, and the faint ding-ding-ding of the car reminding the driver to fasten their seat belt when the car was turned on. His voice over the phone as he yelled, "Run! Just head to the town square. I'll come get you!" The incredibly loud sound of one of the heavy wooden doors slamming shut once she was outside, a vague thought in her mind of how much force would need to be applied to *slam* such a door, an action she never imagined being possible. The cold stone of the veranda on her hands as she caught herself when she fell, followed by the sound of Dr. Bachmann's panicked voice growing softer as the phone fell several feet away. That low, hoarse voice whispering into her ear, "*Go!*"

Not knowing why, she grabbed her phone and ran. As she ran away from the house, the knot of her belt coming loose so the robe now flowed around her, she felt a force on her back that felt like a human hand *pushing* her to go faster.

Once she was on the road that led from Blairmont Manor to the Daffodil town square, she saw headlights as a car came around a curve and sped toward her. With a screeching halt, it stopped beside her, and she got in as quickly as she could.

Dr. Bachmann turned the steering wheel as he reversed the car and then sped off toward town.

Thia, who was not at all athletic, panted as she tried to catch her breath. The ding-ding-ding of the car brought her to her senses, and she reached for the seat belt and fastened it.

"Thank you," she was finally able to say in breathy words as she heaved.

"Breathe," he said. "Take slow, deep breaths."

Thia followed his instructions as he said, "Inhale, two, three, four. Exhale, two, three, four," repeating the instructions several times as they crossed the empty town square.

Once she was calm, Thia looked around, thinking about this unbelievable situation she was in. "Dr. Bachmann," she asked, nearly in tears for fear and bewilderment, "what is happening to me?"

Expecting an explanation full of psychiatric jargon, for she was sure she had just experienced an intense psychotic episode, and feeling safe now to be in the care of a professional, Thia was dismayed to hear him reply, "You just made contact with your roommate."

"I live alone," she reminded him.

"Not according to what everyone in this town believes."

"Are you serious," she asked in an accusatory tone, sharp with anger. "You want to tell me a ghost did this." She wished she had been able to call the other psychiatrist, the real one that she had met with first, but she had not given Thia an emergency contact number. Perhaps she should have called 911 instead. She had nothing with her except her pajamas, her robe, her house shoes, and her phone. Fearful, now, that this "psychiatrist" was a kidnapping con man, if not just a fraud, she asked, "Where are you taking me?"

Noting the panic in her voice, Dr. Bachmann said reassuringly, "I will take you wherever you would like to go. Just tell me where."

Hearing the sincerity in his voice, Thia calmed down and reminded herself that her thoughts of paranoia were caused by stress and that she had to keep her symptoms in check. She thought through her options. She did not want to wake any of her friends, nor did she want to tell them about what was happening to her. And her mother was already so worried about her that she wanted her to move back home, so she definitely could not tell her about this until it was over and figured out.

"I have nowhere to go," she finally said.

Dr. Bachmann was silent for a moment. Then, he said, "I guess I could find a hotel for you. I'm sorry I don't know anyone who would take you in. It's not you, I hope you understand, it's what they think you might bring with you into their homes. Everyone in Daffodil thinks Blairmont Manor is haunted."

After a few moments of silence, he asked, "How would you feel about staying in the waiting room of my office?"

"Alone?" Thia asked, suddenly aware that she was afraid of her own company, that she did not trust herself or her own perception and sense of reality.

"It's already very unprofessional of me to let you stay in the waiting room of my office outside of work hours. It would be crossing another line entirely to stay with you overnight. You can figure out a plan in the morning, somewhere to stay until you find a new home, call Carol to get Blairmont back on the market and—"

"*What?*" Thia asked.

As he pulled into the driveway of his bungalow, he said, "I'm going to get some blankets and pillows, and then I'll be right back to take you to my office."

"You're not leaving me alone."

"Thia," he said, "you cannot come into my house."

"I cannot remain alone unmedicated in this psychotic state."

He sighed, and she was infuriated that he still did not believe her.

"I am convinced someone was in my house, even though my eyes saw no one, and I am convinced I *felt* someone touch me and *heard* someone talk to me." Then, she added, "And I'm not really your patient, right? You never prescribed medication for me, nor did we have a real session. All you did was give Dr. Sherman the assurance he demanded to fill my prescription from my real psychiatrist."

"The lines of professionalism are not that blurry," he said. "Not to me anyway."

"Then why did you pick me up in your car in the middle of the night instead of telling me to call 911?"

Seeing her point and seeing that it was largely his fault that she was at his house and in this situation, without any form of identification or money or even real clothes, he said, "Okay, come on in."

She followed him up the few wooden steps to his front porch. He opened the front door—it was already unlocked—and turned on a light.

"You can stay here," he said, having thought it through. "But only for tonight."

"Thank you," she said.

He got some blankets and an extra pillow from a closet in the hallway. Thia put the pillow at one end of the couch in the living room and spread out a blanket.

"Do you want to talk about what happened?" he asked.

"Are you going to try to convince me it was a ghost?"

He nodded.

"Then, no," Thia replied, "I do not want to talk about it. I just want to sleep it off and see how I feel in the morning. I'll call my psychiatrist as soon as her office opens tomorrow."

"Thia, just hear me out," Dr. Bachmann tried.

But Thia would hear nothing of it. "Do you have a sleeping pill or something I can take?" she asked. "I won't be able to sleep without one."

After a long pause, Dr. Bachmann asked, "When did you take the most recent dose of your current medication?"

"This morning," Thia said, then corrected herself, "yesterday morning, I guess. I would take the next dose in a few hours."

He left, and she heard the sounds in another room of a cabinet being unlocked, opened, and then shut and locked. He then returned and walked across the living room to the kitchen to get a glass of water.

Handing her the glass of water and a pill, he said, "I keep a small supply of tranquilizers, antipsychotics, and sleep aids, in case of emergencies. You can take this to help you sleep tonight."

"Is it okay to take with my other medication?" Thia asked.

"This won't interact with it. And your dose isn't large enough to cause any problems if you stop taking it."

"Thank you," Thia said, taking the pill and glass of water from him. She put the pill in her mouth and swallowed it right away.

"Okay," Dr. Bachmann said, still uneasy about having Thia stay overnight at his house. He made it a point to keep strict boundaries with anyone he treated, official patient or not. "Light on or off?" he asked.

"On, if that's okay," Thia said, now painfully aware of the situation. She closed her robe around herself and tied the belt.

"Okay, well, if there's nothing else—"

"I'll be fine," Thia said, the pill taking effect and embarrassment enveloping her.

"Okay, I'll be in that room down the hall if you need anything," he said, gesturing toward the bedroom.

"Thank you," she said again.

Thia heard him walk the short distance to the bedroom and shut the door. She sat down on the couch, a wave of exhaustion passing over her. She barely covered herself with the second blanket before falling fast asleep.

THIA WOKE TO THE SOUND AND SMELL OF COFFEE being brewed in the kitchen. As she came out of the fog in her mind, from being fully asleep to being fully awake, the memories of the previous evening, or rather only snippets thereof, came back to her.

She folded the blankets and set them on the couch and then removed the pillowcase from the pillow and set it on top of the blankets.

Behind her, Dr. Bachmann said, "Good morning."

Thia turned around and saw him standing in the dining area next to the small kitchen.

"Sorry if I woke you," he said. "I have a session at eight."

Thia looked at the clock on the wall. It was seven-thirty.

"Do you remember what happened last night?" he asked.

"Yes," Thia said, regaining her composure. "Thank you for letting me stay here."

"Would you like some coffee? I made extra."

"Yes, thank you."

"The bathroom's just in the hallway," he said before disappearing around the corner.

After using the restroom, she joined him in the kitchen.

Handing her a mug of coffee, he asked, "Cream and sugar?"

"Yes, please," Thia said.

He got sugar from a cabinet, a spoon from a drawer, and creamer from the refrigerator and set them on the counter for her.

They were silent as Thia added sugar and cream to her coffee. Finally, he said, "I can take you somewhere before work, if you'd like. Or if you'd prefer, someone can pick you up here before I head out." He checked his watch.

"If you wouldn't mind just dropping me off at home, that would be fine."

"You're going back to Blairmont?" he asked.

"Why wouldn't I?" Thia asked.

"Do you remember last night?" he asked her again.

"Mostly," she said. "I'll call my psychiatrist when I get home. Hopefully, she can see me today or at least increase my dosage."

With a tone of authority, Dr. Bachmann looked her directly in the eyes and said, "Thia, you did not have a psychotic episode last night. Everything that happened to you was real."

Thia just stared back at him. She did not know how to respond to that. Finally, she asked, "You really believe ghosts are haunting my house?"

"Ghost," he said. "Just one. And as difficult as it is for me to admit, based on what I've seen—not only with you but with others who have tried to live in that house, too—yes, I do think that."

Thia laughed lightly with disbelief and incredulity. "I'm sorry," she said. "I don't mean to laugh at you. It's just unbelievable to me that a psychiatrist would say that. Look, I don't know what your endgame is, but I thank you for your concern, and I think it's best if I go home now. I can walk. It's not that far."

"No," he said, holding his hand out, palm down, near her but not touching her or physically stopping her from leaving. "I'll drive you." He checked his watch and added, "There's plenty of time if we leave now." Retrieving his keys, phone, and wallet from a table next to the front door, he continued, "But I think you should talk to someone."

Following him out the front door and to his car, Thia said, "Yes, I promise to call my doctor as soon as I get home."

"No," he said, "I'm not talking about a psychiatrist. I'm talking about a historian." He pulled a folded sheet of paper out of his pocket and gave it to her.

They got into his car, and he backed out of the driveway.

As Thia unfolded the paper and read the name, location, and phone number, Dr. Bachmann explained, "He's a professor at the university and has done extensive research on the region and is something of an expert when it comes to Blairmont Manor."

To appease him, and for that reason only, Thia thanked him and promised she would call the professor.

"Go see him today," Dr. Bachmann said. "I'll go with you, if you'd like."

"No, thank you," Thia said, trying not to sound too obvious that she was feeling a little smothered by his insistence. Having thought the situation through—being driven in a car by a psychiatrist who thought she was perfectly mentally healthy, despite her hallucinations and delusional thoughts, and on top of it thought her house was haunted—she decided the best thing she could do now was to oblige him until they parted ways, after which she hoped to never see him again. "I'll give him a call."

"He has a lot of records he could show you," Dr. Bachmann continued. "You wanted to open the house for tours, right? He can help you with that."

His house being just on the other side of the town square, they had reached Blairmont Manor and were parked in front of the veranda. He shut off the engine and unbuckled his seat belt.

"You don't need to come in," Thia said.

Cautiously, he said, "If it's okay with you, I'd feel better if I accompanied you. I can stay in the living room or kitchen while you get dressed and get your things."

This whole time, Thia realized, he had assumed she was going to move out, like everyone suggested, and that she only wanted to come home this morning so she could quickly get a few belongings before leaving again. She took a deep breath and tried to think of what she could say to get rid of him, laughing in the back of her mind at how similar this situation was to the times when she tried to get rid of Millie and Herschel, who still stuck around. The people in this town were nothing if not persistent.

"Thank you for your concern, but I'll be okay."

"I think I should come in to make sure nothing happens to you, though. It would make me feel better."

"I'll take my medication, as long as it's okay. I think the effects of the sleeping pill haven't worn off yet because I feel very calm and relaxed. You would think I'd be scared to come back, but everything will be fine once my doctor gets the dosage figured out."

"I wasn't talking about a psychotic episode."

"You're talking about the ghost, aren't you?"

He nodded.

"What makes you think nothing will happen to you?"

He looked at the house and said, "I think I have a deeper relationship with this ghost than what would appear on the surface. She always seems to avoid me or do things to my patients that end up making *me* look bad." He looked at Thia. "I think her goal is to make the shrink look crazy."

"It's working," Thia assured him, and they both laughed.

"How many previous owners of Blairmont have you treated?" Thia asked, still trying to figure out the scheme he and Dr. Sherman had set up. Then, realizing what she had just asked, she quickly added, "If you're allowed to tell me."

"Zero," he said. "It's the people she doesn't regularly torment and blackmail and extort who have a hard time believing it and end up coming to me. From what I understand, the owners get the message fairly quickly and leave."

"You're not going to leave me here alone, are you?"

He shook his head.

After another moment, she finally gave in. "Okay, you can come in and wait while I get dressed. And then I'll go see this historian."

10

Knocking on the open door, Thia addressed an older man sitting at a cluttered desk, surrounded by stacks of papers and books. "Dr. Manning?"

The man looked up from his work. "Yes?"

"Hi, I'm Thia Watkins. We spoke on the phone?"

"Yes, come in!" He stood up and used both hands to lift a large stack of papers off of a chair. Placing the stack of papers on top of a stack of books, he said, "Sorry, I wasn't expecting you so soon. Please, sit down."

As Thia made her way to the chair, she said, "Yes, I'm sorry to just show up like this. I was in kind of an odd situation this morning, where I was basically forced to come here right away." Then, remembering her manners, she quickly added, "Not that I didn't want to come. It's just that I normally would have set up an appointment. We can do that now, if you'd like, and I can come back later."

"No, not at all! I'm delighted to get to talk with you. I don't often get to talk about Winifred."

"I'm sorry," Thia said, "I'm not here to talk about whoever that is. I'm here to learn more about the history of the area. You see, I'm in the process of getting my home on the national registry as a historic landmark, and I'm seeking information I can include when I open it for tours."

"Sorry, I must have you confused with someone else. What house is it that you are going to open to the public? I know about them all!"

The man was clearly passionate. It was refreshing to see someone as excited about his work as Thia was about hers. Having been perked up by his energy, Thia replied with enthusiasm, "Blairmont Manor!"

After a quick raise of his eyebrows, Dr. Manning said, "Then you are who I thought you were. And we can't talk about Blairmont Manor without talking about Winifred."

"Who?" Thia asked, but as she asked, the landline on his desk began to ring.

"Sorry, one second," he said to her. He picked up the phone and said, "Hello?"

Thia looked down at her hands in her lap, not wanting to eavesdrop but also not wanting to look at anything else in the room so as not to appear to be snooping. "Oh yeah, that's right…Yes, you'll have to teach it. I'm in a meeting," she heard him say. "Just tell them you'll be right back, and you can swing by here for my notes. Hurry."

He hung up the phone and laughed as he said to Thia, "That was my grad student, calling to ask how late I would be to the class I'm supposed to be teaching right now."

"I'm so sorry," Thia said, beginning to stand up. "I'll come back after your class."

"No, no, this is much more important. The truth is, I totally forgot about it once I got the call from your friend saying you were coming here to talk about Winifred. Like I said, I rarely get to talk about her."

"Yes, about Winifr—" Thia started, but she was interrupted by a panting, sweating guy, bursting into the room.

Dr. Manning shuffled some papers around on his desk and then handed a few sheets of notepad paper, full of handwritten notes, to the guy, who Thia could only assume was the graduate student. With a quick "Thanks," he left as quickly as he had appeared.

"Yes, Winifred," Dr. Manning said excitedly, returning his attention to Thia.

"I'm sorry, I don't know who that is."

"Your resident ghost," he said.

Thia's heart sank. "I'm sorry," she said again. "I don't believe in ghosts. I was hoping to get information about the house, though, and the area."

"You haven't had *any* odd encounters or strange occurrences in the house?" he asked.

Thia took a deep breath and said, "No." Then, after he gave her a look of skepticism, she quickly added, "Not like that. Not anything *paranormal*, per se."

Up to this point, Dr. Manning had been leaning over his desk, eager to speak with her. Now, he leaned back in his chair, content to listen to her stories. "Tell me," he said.

She told him about the gate, about Millie and Herschel, about furniture being moved and the sheets being changed.

"That's not so scary," he said.

"Well…" Thia started.

He leaned forward again and placed his clasped hands on the desk. "*Yes…?*"

"There have been other things, but I have explanations for them."

"And they are…?"

"Well, at first, my business notebook kept disappearing, even though I was the only person in the house. Later, I thought someone broke into my home. When I went to the town hall meeting, I found out the town gets the commission each time Blairmont Manor is sold. So, my theory is that they are trying to scare me into leaving so that I sell Blairmont, and then they will get the commission."

"And what have they been doing to scare you?" he asked.

"Well," Thia said again, taking a breath. She told him about the bells that went missing and about how the security cameras conveniently malfunctioned just long enough for the culprit to remain anonymous.

As she spoke, Dr. Manning listened intently, eyebrows raised, a small delighted smile of amusement forming on his lips.

"That's it?" he asked.

"What else would there be?" she asked.

"Objects moving by themselves. Strange or inexplicable sounds. A voice or low laughter, like she's trying to hold it in but can't help herself. You haven't seen a woman? Either in form or in a reflection?"

Thia sat still, dumbfounded.

"You have," he said with a smile.

"I'm sorry," Thia said, shaking her head. "I just don't believe in ghosts." She did not want to insult him, but there was nothing else to say.

He stood up and said, "Come with me."

She followed him as he led her through the building, out across the quad, and to a library.

As they walked, he asked, "How long have you owned Blairmont?"

"About two months," Thia replied.

"And how often have you been inside the house?"

"I live there," Thia replied.

He stopped and looked at her. "You've been living in the house for two months?"

Thia nodded.

"Huh," he said and continued to walk. "I wonder why she has allowed you to stick around for so long."

"Two months is a long time?" Thia asked.

"It is when you live there. Most people don't *live* at Blairmont, they vacation there, so it's rare that they are physically in the house long enough to make her mad and drive them out. And as long as they stay out of her way and obey the rules, she allows them to be there for a day or two at a time, such as over a weekend. But anyone who is there longer than a week usually ends up fleeing, too scared to return."

"What do you mean by staying out of her way? And what are the rules?"

"From what I understand, she treats the house as if it is hers," he replied. They had reached a door to one of the university's libraries. Before opening it, he stopped and looked at Thia. "And she gets nasty when she does not get her way."

He swung the door open and held it for Thia. He then led her through the maze of rooms and rows of shelves, from the beautiful entrance and showy reading rooms, to the more functionally designed, less aesthetic rooms, and then finally to a room for which he had to swipe his faculty ID card to enter.

They were immediately greeted not by a student worker but by an older librarian behind a desk. Thia knew they were about to enter a room of great importance when Dr.

Manning signed a logbook with his name, faculty number, the date and time, and a request for which materials he wanted to view. He then told the librarian why they were there and what items they wanted to see. The librarian disappeared for several minutes and returned with a large box, which he handed to Dr. Manning over the counter. Dr. Manning thanked the librarian and led Thia to a table.

Opening the box, he said, "These have been digitized, so I could have shown you this on the computer in my office, but I prefer to look at the original documents." He pulled out a chair to take a seat. Pulling a large, old book out of the box, he said, "There's something about holding it in your hands and feeling the pages as you turn them with your fingers that connects you with the past, knowing these same pages have been touched by so many others, including the ones who wrote what we are about to read."

He pulled out the chair next to him and patted it. "Sit," he told her.

Thia sat next to him, and he slid the book toward the center so they could both see it. Opening it, he said, "This is the original ledger of Blairmont Manor." The book contained handwritten dated entries with the expenses for food, labor, and items bought for the house.

Thia's eyes brightened as he turned the pages. "This is one of the coolest things I have ever seen in my life," she said.

He smiled, delighted, and said, "I thought you would think so. The last owner of Blairmont who came to see me— that was nearly a decade ago, mind you—said the same thing. And I thought the same thing the first time I held it, too…although I think the word I used back then was 'tubular.'"

Thia laughed and asked, "What got you interested in Blairmont? Did you grow up knowing about it?" She had assumed so because the only people she knew who knew about Blairmont were the townspeople of Daffodil.

"No," he said, no longer turning the pages. "I grew up out west and had planned on going to college in the northeast to major in ancient history and study the classics. But I took a year off after high school to travel, and my first goal was to hike the Appalachian Trail. Well, I fell in love with the area and never left." He sat up and turned toward her. "In fact, I spent every summer as a volunteer, maintaining different parts of the Trail up until a few years ago."

"That's really impressive!"

"Have you hiked it?" he asked.

"No," Thia said. "I've never been much of a camper or backpacker, although I do like to go on walks in the woods and in parks. I've lived in the city for most of my life, until I moved to Blairmont."

"It was the A.T. that brought me here, and I applied to colleges in Virginia, Tennessee, North Carolina, and South Carolina, and then went on to get my doctorate, focusing on regional history." He paused and then said with a satisfied smile, "And I've been researching it ever since."

"It's inspiring to meet someone so passionate about their work," Thia said.

"I've been very lucky," he said, turning back to the book. "Now, here is where the real story begins."

Thia leaned over so she could see what he was pointing at on the page.

"The first sale of Blairmont Manor," he said. "You can see the handwriting is different. The second owner continued to use this book for his accounts with the house, likely so he could compare rates he was being given with those that were given to the previous owner for negotiations. But what is so interesting about this is the year that it was sold." He pushed the book across the table to make room and pulled a binder out of the box, placing it on the table in front of them where the ledger had been. "The tycoon who built Blairmont Manor had a son who was supposed to inherit it."

He carefully opened the binder. Inside were newspaper clippings and photographs encased in thick, clear protective sleeves. The first item was a newspaper article about the death of the son.

"He killed himself?" Thia asked, heartbroken for the family. "Do you know why?"

Dr. Manning turned the page to reveal another newspaper clipping, this one about the drowning of a young bride.

"How awful," Thia said, reading in the article that this drowned woman, Mary Stinson, had just married the heir to Blairmont at a church in town, which Thia assumed was no longer there because she was not familiar with it. The reception for the wedding had taken place at Blairmont Manor. And it was in the lake at Blairmont where she had drowned. Thia looked at Dr. Manning and asked, "So is that why he killed himself? Out of grief?"

"It's not known for sure, but that's the assumption." He turned back to the previous article, the one about the son, and pointed at the date. Then, he reached across the table to point at the year of the sale in the ledger. "After the death of his only son, he sold Blairmont. The hauntings started around this time, too." He pulled another book out of the box, this one an old journal. "The first hauntings are recorded here." He turned to a page and showed it to Thia.

As she started reading, he said, "You won't be able to tell they're hauntings from that entry. But there's a pattern. Over time, the writer of that journal came to believe the incidents were occurring as the result of a 'supernatural force,' as he called it."

"So, that's why people think the house is haunted, because the son and his wife died there," Thia concluded.

"Partly," he said. "We don't have *all* the documentation here,"—he placed a hand on the box as he said the word "here"—"but I've pieced together quite a bit by visiting other libraries and archives." He returned to the binder and flipped the pages to show another newspaper clipping, this one about a public lynching. "This is the woman who is believed to haunt the house: Winifred Byrne."

Thia skimmed the title and article. "She was lynched ahead of her trial?"

"Very rare, for a woman to be lynched. But the town was angry."

Thia looked at him, knowing he was about to tell her the story that he said he had pieced together.

"This woman," he said, placing an index finger on the article, "was a servant in the house of Mary Stinson, the bride who was later found dead. Now, through journal entries and interviews and hearing stories told through generations, it seems that she was insanely jealous of Mary because she was in love with the heir to Blairmont. There was even a rumor that this servant girl had an affair with him, but I'm inclined to believe that is entirely made up and that she may have started the rumor herself as a way to cause a scandal that would lead to canceling the wedding.

Ultimately, she was accused of killing Mary—that's the bride and the daughter of the people she worked for. If you look at the dates of the deaths"—he turned the pages so she could see the dates of the articles—"it would appear as though it was his suicide that angered the mob so much that they lynched her."

"She was accused, but she was never convicted?" Thia asked. Although she was not a believer in ghosts, to hear him tell the story was captivating. In fact, it was kind of fun to talk about it like this. She considered how it might affect the business if she included a ghost story in her marketing materials. People could see for themselves if Blairmont was haunted, and if so, who they thought was haunting it. "Maybe that's why she's stuck at Blairmont." Then, remembering herself, she felt obligated to explain, "Because they say if a ghost is here, it's because something is keeping the soul from moving on. Maybe she was innocent and can't fully 'rest in peace,' so to speak, until her name is cleared."

"It's a good theory," he agreed, "but it's not the impression I get from the encounters."

As he pulled another large book from the box, Thia asked, "Then what's keeping her there? Why can't she leave Blairmont?"

"Oh, she's not bound to the house," he said. "She can go wherever she wants. She does, according to the locals whom she terrorizes and extorts. She could be sitting at this table with us right now, for all I know."

As he opened the latest book he had pulled out, Thia gave a glance to each of the other, presumably empty, chairs at their table.

"The last entry in here is from nearly a decade ago, written by that last owner I mentioned, who came to see me.

I would appreciate it if you would add your stories, too." He had opened the book to the next blank page and placed it in front of her. Then, he took a pen from his shirt pocket and held it out toward her.

"But I don't have any stories to tell," Thia stated.

"Anything peculiar you can think of, whether you think it was Winifred or not," he said.

"I'm sorry," Thia apologized, "but hasn't this poor woman been through enough? Not the supposed ghost, but *this woman.*" She pointed at the article in the binder that was still open on the table. "She was a real person, and she was accused of killing someone. Now, she's accused of terrorizing people today, and she has no way to defend herself against any of these charges. And if I put my stories in here, future generations will assume that *I* thought she was real, which I don't, and after I'm gone, I won't be able to defend myself either."

"Then put that in here," he said. "You can write whatever you want. The important thing is to have the owners of Blairmont Manor share their experiences. If you don't have any paranormal incidents to share, that's just as important because it lets us know that there were people who lived in Blairmont without any problems at all."

"Well..." Thia hesitated before continuing. "It's not that *nothing* has happened, it's just that I don't think it was supernatural. I think all the things that I've experienced were caused by living humans." *Or were made up in my mind,* she added to herself in her head. She did not want to tell him about her hallucinations.

"Then, please," he said, "put that in here. Maybe it is a living person doing this. Anything you write will serve as another piece to the puzzle that I, and any future researchers, can use to figure out what is going on at that mansion."

Thia thumbed through the corners of the previous pages, feeling each one pass over her thumb, feeling just how many pages had been filled with stories. "Is it okay if I read previous entries?" she asked.

"I'd prefer it if you wrote yours first, so you're not subconsciously influenced by the others. Even if you didn't intend to write similar—or different—accounts, reading what others wrote might cause you to put a different spin on your experiences than how they had originally affected you. Right now, you're convinced it is someone specific, a living person; reading the accounts of others may make you write your account in a way that would be even more biased toward it being a person—or less, if reading their accounts convinces you it is Winifred."

Thia looked at the blank page before her, considering it. After a heavy moment, she again glanced at the presumably empty chairs at their table and picked up the pen.

Dr. Manning pointed at the top right corner of the page and said, "Put today's date here."

Thia wrote the date in the top right corner. Then, she wrote, "*My name is Thia (Cynthia) Watkins, and since moving to Blairmont Manor two months ago, I have heard creaking sounds and other little 'pops.' I'm sure these can be attributed to the structure of the house responding to changes in atmospheric pressure because I moved in at the end of summer. I have also heard footsteps in hallways, and when I go into a room, I will notice that things have been moved since the last time I was there. These are likely attributed to Millie, the housekeeper, or others she has brought with her to clean and maintain the property.*"

As she handed the pen back to Dr. Manning, he said,

"Thank you. I really appreciate it." He set the pen on the table and pulled yet another large book out of the box. "If you'd like to add more, you are more than welcome to do so. In fact, I'll probably ask you to again before we leave. But please make a note that whatever you write was after you read the other stories." He handed her the book.

"What's this?" she asked.

"The first official volume of personal accounts."

Thia slid the book she had written in, apparently the second volume, to the side to make room for the new book. She carefully opened the old book and began reading. The first entry was dated a little over a century prior, and the earliest accounts, presumably by people who had known or had seen Winifred, claimed the ghost looked like her.

Thia read one description by a priest who visited to bless the house but was unable to do so because of her presence. It read, *"She wears no bonnet in death but keeps her hair fastened as if she were the mistress of the house, the rightful Lady of Blairmont the spiteful girl always wanted to be. She wears the blue dress she wore when she was hanged. Her skin is as pale as a corpse, and her eyes are sunken in their sockets, but the likeness is unmistakable in those cold, venomous eyes, though she is now a spectre, as fierce and deadly a gaze as she had when she was living. Winifred haunts this house."*

"That poor woman," Thia whispered.

"What?" Dr. Manning asked, amused.

"This is such a mean description of her. Clearly, this priest was very biased."

Dr. Manning shrugged and laughed. "You're the first person to feel *sorry* for Winifred."

Thia continued reading, mostly scanning. Some were personal accounts. Some were posthumously added by others who claimed the deceased had told them the stories. Some were loose sheets of paper inserted between the pages, accounts from other journals that had been photocopied and added to fit the chronology. One disquieting fact that Thia could not ignore was that the accounts, despite occurring over a period of years with multiple owners and witnesses, were similar to what she had experienced herself: the insistence that everything remain the same and that nothing was to be added or removed or relocated; the low, hollow laughter; a woman's voice, whispering in an ear; the appearance of a person in the dark and reflections in glass. Others, still, were far worse than what Thia had experienced: objects moving in the air without any person there to move them, physical attacks that resulted in serious injuries, even one that had led to death.

She moved on to the next book, the one in which she had added her own personal account. As she flipped through the pages, an entry recorded on April 9, 1962, caught her attention:

"The Rules of Living with The Ghost of Blairmont Manor

1 - Everything is to remain exactly where it is, including all the furniture and objects in the house as well as all the plants in the gardens. If any pieces or objects are damaged, they must be repaired and restored to their original condition. If any part of the house needs repairing, it must be repaired to its original condition. If any plants in the gardens die, they must be replaced with the same species in the exact same location.

2 - All changes, repairs, or renovations must first be approved by The Ghost. If she is not first consulted, all changes must be undone so that everything is in its original condition.

3 - All living beings must stay out of the way of The Ghost. In general, humans are confined to the servants' quarters and passages, the gatekeeper's house, and the carriage house. The ballroom, the conservatory, and the bedrooms on the third floor of the south wing are especially prohibited, as this is where she spends most of her time.

4 - The gate at the entrance, next to the gatekeeper's house, and all doors of the main house leading to the outside are to remain closed and locked.

5 - Although The Ghost prefers to stay in the house, and even when the above rules are obeyed, she may be upset when anyone is anywhere in the house or on the property if her mood is ill tempered. Be warned that she is moody, cantankerous, malicious, and easily angered.

The above rules were not given to me by The Ghost but were deduced by myself through experience and trial and error."

A note followed the above rules, dated April 17, 1962, stating, *"Now deceased. It is advised not to try to follow any 'rules' and to instead avoid setting foot on the property of Blairmont Manor at all costs, unless absolutely necessary."* Whoever had written the note did not sign it.

Turning from the book and looking at Dr. Manning, Thia asked, "And you think all of these are attributed to the ghost? This one ghost in particular? This one woman, at that?"

"Personally, I can't say," he responded. "But it is interesting, isn't it?"

"Where did these books come from?" Thia asked.

"The town council kept them in the town hall up until 1992, when I convinced them to have them stored here with other important items for historical research. I suppose it helped that the old hag tried to burn down the town hall—or at least it helped that the town council believed that at the time. The fire started in the room where these journals and ledgers were kept, having been given to the town council for safekeeping in 1963. From what I understand, it is believed that something was written in there that upset her, leading her to want to destroy them, and then something upset her again in 1992."

"But what happened?" Thia asked. "What made her so angry those two times?"

He shrugged with a smile. He was having the time of his life talking about this. Meanwhile, Thia was only more confused by it all.

"And what do you know about this Winifred person who has been accused of haunting Blairmont? Do you know anything about her, other than that she was accused of killing Mary Stinson and lynched for it before there was a proper trial, conviction, and sentencing?"

"Only that she had a reputation for being a troublemaker."

"How old was she?"

"Her age when she died is unknown, but I think somewhere around twenty or in her late teens."

Thia looked at the article about the lynching again. The whole town had shown up for it, and yet not a single person was ever charged or prosecuted for her death.

"So?" Dr. Manning asked. "Do you want to add more to your account, now that you've had a chance to see what others wrote before you?"

"Maybe another time," Thia said. "This is a lot to take in. But you said this was digitized. Can I have the files so I can read these later?"

"They belong to the university, so I'm afraid you need to be affiliated to access them. But"—he did a quick glance-around—"nothing is stopping you from taking pictures with your phone."

"Are you sure?" Thia asked.

He shrugged. "As the owner of Blairmont, I think you should have access to these. If someone gets mad about it, you can delete the photos."

Thia pulled out her phone and took a picture of the three articles, the one about Mary Stinson's death, the heir to Blairmont's suicide, and Winifred's lynching. She also took a photo of the "rules." She flipped through more pages and asked, "Why didn't the town council tell me about this? Why didn't anyone tell me about any of this?"

"From what I understand, Winifred has a tight gag order on everyone. She seems to run the town in that sense. And as long as she gets her way, there is peace in Daffodil."

Ridiculous, Thia thought, mindful of what her psychiatrist had told her about her anxiety inducing symptoms of paranoia, and she tried to keep the thoughts of delusional thinking and conspiracies in check. But to her, this seemed like a very convenient story the town council could use in achieving their goal of selling Blairmont Manor every few years. That they had convinced the whole town to believe this was further injustice as far as Thia was concerned.

She continued to scan more entries. In the 1970's, Herschel's name appeared, and after a few more pages, Millie's name caught her eye, too, dated in the late 1990's. She turned to the entry on the page before hers, dated nine years and three months earlier. It read, *"I bought Blairmont Manor four months ago. After several failed attempts to renovate and too many strange and spooky experiences, I have decided to sell it. Let someone else deal with this mess."*

"Well, he had a terrible attitude," Thia said after reading it.

"He was fascinating," Dr. Manning said. "He had many plans for Blairmont. He wanted to entirely transform the interior. Like you, he thought there had to be a non-paranormal explanation, until he saw a hammer picked up off the floor by an unseen entity and hurled through the air to hit one of the contractors."

Thia's eyes widened. "Was the contractor okay?"

"I don't remember," Dr. Manning responded. "That was only one of many stories. He did not want to write any of them down. They were too painful."

He reached into his pocket and pulled out a folded sheet of paper. "I know you are still skeptical, Ms. Watkins, but I would recommend that you get in contact with one of these paranormal investigators. As the rightful owner of Blairmont Manor, you alone have the power to get rid of her." He handed her the piece of paper containing a handwritten list of names and phone numbers. "The last owner I spoke to, as you can tell from his entry, was unwilling to try and just wanted to be rid of the whole ordeal. But you seem like you want to stay there. This may be your only way of doing that."

"Thank you," Thia said, taking the sheet of paper from

him and putting it in her purse. "And thank you for showing me all of this. It was really neat, and if it's okay with you, I'd love to come back some time and talk more about the house."

"Any time!" he said.

"And feel free to come to Blairmont Manor," Thia said, closing the books and binder. "I plan on opening it to the public very soon."

"I sincerely hope you do," Dr. Manning replied.

AFTER A LATE LUNCH IN THE CITY WITH MONICA and Ruth, following her long, unexpected morning with Dr. Manning, Thia returned to Blairmont Manor and sat at the large antique desk in the office to work on her plans for the gradual opening. She would start with making the bedrooms available for overnight guests. Then, she would open the ballroom and conservatory and other areas for private events, followed by opening a restaurant that would serve tables in the large dining hall, and then having daily tours. Her phone sat next to her purse at one end of the desk, but she was too focused on her work to notice the screen brighten as it was unlocked and as the photo gallery was opened.

She had devised a better schedule that would allow her to open even sooner than she had expected and was in the process of writing it out when she heard a quick whisking sound behind her, followed by a low hiss. She turned around to see that the gas logs in the large marble fireplace had been turned on. Then, she watched as the folded sheet of paper Dr. Manning had given her slowly emerged from her purse, as if being pulled out by an invisible hand. Suspended in the air, the paper was slowly, as if to be intentionally dramatic, unfolded and then floated across the room to the fire. The sheet of paper was not thrown into the fire, but hovered over the flames, as if held there, so only the corner was lit.

Thia quickly stood up and looked around the room, hoping for an explanation, but found none. The sheet of paper, aflame now, slowly floated back toward her. Then, it stopped, directly in front of her at eye level, the slow line of the charred edge rising toward the top as the consumed portion disappeared into ash and drifted to the floor. When all the names and numbers had been destroyed, with only the university letterhead at the top remaining, the paper was crumpled up, still in the air, so as to put out the flame. The crumpled paper then dropped onto the desk, landing directly on top of the new soft opening schedule she had been working on.

"Okay," Thia whispered, slowly coming to her senses and trying to think of even the slightest reasonable explanation for what had just occurred. Coming up with nothing, she looked at the empty air around her and asked, "Hello?"

She picked up her phone to call Dr. Bachmann. Upon touching it, the screen went from the blank, black screen to what had most recently been accessed. Thia saw the picture she had taken of "The Rules of Living with The Ghost of Blairmont Manor," zoomed in on rule number three, where it stated that humans were confined to the servants' quarters.

"Okay," Thia said, taking the hint. She told the empty room, "I'll do my work in the servants' quarters from now on."

Quickly, she gathered her purse, her phone, and all her business materials—feeling simultaneously foolish for even considering she might be talking to a ghost and equally as foolish for not believing Dr. Bachmann, Dr. Manning, and all the accounts she had read earlier that day.

She hurriedly turned off the gas logs and then the lamp on the desk. As soon as the light was off, the figure of a woman appeared, standing before her.

Like all the other times this had happened, Thia quickly turned the light back on to convince her mind that it was not real, that there was nobody there, that she really was alone in the room.

But this time the figure did not disappear.

11

"SKIN AS PALE AS A CORPSE. EYES SUNKEN IN THEIR sockets." The description was spot on. She even wore a blue dress. But the gaze, which Thia remembered reading as being fierce and deadly, was downright malevolent.

She hovered in the air, her feet inches above the floor, her form appearing mostly solid, with just a touch of being airy and semitransparent, just enough to show she was not entirely of this world, as if she were made of billions of tiny particles all floating in the air in unison. Her skin had a grayish hue with the appearance of being stretched thinly across her brittle bones like taut cellophane, causing her cheekbones to jut out and form unnatural contours on her face. Her hair, pinned up in a Victorian-style bun, was thin and straggly, like long fragile tendrils sitting atop a bare skull. And with the physical manifestation of her ominous presence came a revolting, rancid odor, as if the soul, when detached from its physical counterpart, must also rot and decompose if left on Earth instead of moving on to the spiritual realm.

Frozen with fear, Thia asked, in a shaky, barely audible whisper, "Are you Winifred?"

The ghost slowly glided toward Thia, causing her to

stumble as she took a step back. Thia then moved around the desk and started walking backward toward the door, too frightened to turn her back to the spectral being.

Unconstrained by the laws of physics, the translucent form traversed through the desk and continued advancing forward. In a voice recognizable to Thia as the one she had heard whispering in her ear before, the apparition said, "Never in all my years have I encountered anyone so foolish and dim-witted, so steeped in denial, so barricaded in oblivion, so closed off and unwilling to see what is so *painfully* clear. Never in all my years has it taken *this long* for my presence to *finally* be acknowledged. You mindless, harebrained little girl! Why have you been so preposterous, so headstrong in your insistence I could not exist? Why has it taken you so long? *What is wrong with you?*"

By now, Thia had backed into the wide corridor that spanned the entire length of the south wing. Pointing toward the main entrance, the ghost gave a single command: "*Leave.*"

Unable to speak, Thia nodded and ran as fast as she could, still holding all her belongings from the office, not daring to drop them, lest the ghost get angry with her for leaving her things behind. She struggled to open the large wooden door, but in an instant it easily gave way as the ghost swung the door open, so quickly that Thia had to jump out of the way. Thia ran across the veranda, down the stairs and to her car, opening the passenger side door and tossing all her things onto the seat before running around to the driver's side and getting in. She pressed the button to turn on the engine and stepped on the gas, causing a revving sound as she realized she had not put the car in drive. She quickly did so, and the car leaped forward with a start, sending a piercing cry as she peeled out with a screech of the tires on the driveway. She continued on, speeding away, fastening her seat belt only after she was on the secluded, narrow road to the town square.

Though just a mile, the road had never felt so long, and when she finally came to the end of it, she had to slam on her brakes as she nearly hit a couple carrying lights and streamers. They jumped as she stopped, seeing the fear in her eyes and stepping out of her way as they gave each other a knowing look before daring to look behind her car, down the road toward the ominous and infamous Blairmont Manor.

Thia cautiously continued, all the people stepping out of her way. The small town square, full of locals decorating the streets, lampposts, and storefronts for the upcoming Halloween Festival, seemed to pause in time. Everyone stopped what they were doing, once they saw the car that came from *that road*, the road no one ever dared to go on, and the look on the driver's face, that look they had seen before from drivers in cars that sped away from that house. That look like they had just seen a ghost.

They watched her car go through the square, looked toward the house and that forest that separated the town from *her*, and then around at each other, as if to assess and check on their fellow townspeople, making sure they were each okay, making sure *she* did not follow the car and linger there.

Before she knew where she was going, Thia found herself pulling into the driveway of Dr. Bachmann's bungalow, just on the other side of the small town square. She ran up the wooden steps and across the wooden porch and banged on the front door with the palm of her hand. She was not aware that she was not stopping until the door swung open and she nearly hit Dr. Bachmann in the face.

"I'm sorry," she said, still shaking. "I didn't know where else to go."

"Thia, I can't—" he began.

"I'm not here as a patient," she said quickly, interrupting him.

Seeing the look on her face, his expression softened, and he stepped aside to allow her in.

"I'm sorry," she said again. "It's just—"

"It's okay," he said, understanding. "Take some deep breaths." He closed the door. "Have a seat."

"I saw her," Thia said, barely believing her own words. "I *saw* her. And *smelled* her. It was awful."

She followed him into the living room and sat on the couch.

"I just...I can't...I..." Thia said.

"It's okay," Dr. Bachmann said, sitting next to her.

Looking at Dr. Bachmann, she repeated, "I *saw* her."

Dr. Bachmann nodded.

"It wasn't a hallucination, was it?"

Dr. Bachmann shook his head. Then, he dared to ask, "Is she here now?"

Thia looked around the room and shook her head, but then she shrugged as she looked back at him and said, "The truth is, I don't know. I never saw her until tonight. And she was there the whole time, but I never saw her before. She could be here, couldn't she? Oh my goodness, she could. She was there this whole time. She—"

"Okay," Dr. Bachmann said, urging her to stay calm. "It's okay. She's not here."

"This is unreal. I can't believe what just happened."

"What *did* happen exactly?" Dr. Bachmann asked.

"She…she…" Thia started and then began hyperventilating.

"Okay," Dr. Bachmann said again. "We don't have to talk about it right now." He stood up and told her to lie down with her feet up and to take deep breaths. "I'll make you some hot tea."

He went to the kitchen, and Thia lay on the couch, focusing on taking deep breaths as he had instructed her.

When he came back several minutes later with a mug of hot tea, she sat up and said, "Everyone was right. I have to move out. I should have never moved to Blairmont Manor."

He handed her the mug and said, "It's a good thing you came around. It could have been much worse."

She sat on the edge of the cushion, holding the mug with both hands, staring downward at the floor but not focusing on anything, only gazing distantly at empty space.

"I don't know how. Everything is ready. I finally got everything in place." She looked at him. "I'm ready to open. The permits and licenses have been granted. The website is ready. All my advertising is in place. I was just about to go live with all of it."

"Then it's good you didn't. But it was good practice," he said, trying to look on the bright side. "Now, when you sell Blairmont and buy another place, you will already know exactly what you want and how to get the hotel going."

Thia looked straight ahead without looking at anything in particular, thinking of all the work she would have to do to start over. She would never find another place like Blairmont, a mansion hotel so huge and beautiful, with multiple event spaces to rent out, a lake, and gardens. And with all the rooms already furnished.

Finally, she turned to him and asked, "What will I tell everyone?"

Dr. Bachmann shrugged and said, "Just tell them it didn't work out. They don't have to know the specifics. You don't have to tell anyone. In fact, I'm surprised the ghost didn't order you to stay quiet about it. From what I hear, that's the number one thing she cares about."

"I don't think she even thought about that. She was so *angry* with me. She just wanted me to leave."

"And you did. You did the right thing."

They sat for a moment in silence, and then Thia said, "I can't believe this is real. I thought you were dumb for suggesting it, that everyone in the town was simple for being superstitious, that it was just for fun when Dr. Manning was talking about it."

"Did he have any advice for you?" Dr. Bachmann asked.

"He gave me a list of professionals who could help me get rid of her, exorcise the house or something, I guess—but she burned the list."

"She burned it?"

Thia nodded. "Right in front of me. It was like this terrifying, yet mesmerizing, act. I couldn't see her, only the piece of paper. She pulled it out of my purse and lit it on fire. Then, when I came to my senses, I picked up my notebook and laptop and all my papers and started to leave. And when I turned off the light, she was there. I turned it back on, and she was still there. She told me in so many words that I was stupid and that I was a fool for not seeing her before, and then she told me to leave." She turned to him and asked, "Is that similar to what you've heard from others?"

"Actually, it's fairly mild compared to what I've been told. She didn't threaten you?"

"No!" Thia said, shocked at the idea. "Why do you ask?"

"She usually does, from what I understand. Maybe since you were already leaving, she didn't feel it was necessary. When she doesn't get what she wants, she resorts to making someone's life miserable, doing whatever she has to until she gets her way."

"That's terrible. Is that why Millie and Herschel work for the house?"

"And Carol and others, yes."

"What will she do if they don't do what she wants?"

Dr. Bachmann shook his head. "I don't know. They've never told anyone. But enough people have been threatened by her that they don't need to explain themselves."

"Then why is she still here? Why hasn't someone gotten rid of her? Dr. Manning said that as the rightful owner of the house, I could. Why haven't others before me done that?"

"I think they were so traumatized by their experiences that they just wanted to get away as quickly as possible."

"And what about the town? Why do all these people put up with her? Why haven't they moved?"

"It's been peaceful for years. As long as the ghost is happy, she stays in the house and keeps to herself. It's the people who go in there that she bothers. The town isn't affected unless she's upset and somehow disrupting the lives of others will help her get what she wants."

"I can't believe I'm having this conversation," she said, still in shock.

Dr. Bachmann laughed. "I know." He stood up and walked toward the hall closet. "Stay here tonight. Call Carol in the morning. She'll help you move out and get things going. She's well aware of the process by now. She's probably expecting your call."

"She is," Thia said, laughing slightly. "She told me right after I moved in to call her when I decided to sell. I thought she was joking."

Dr. Bachmann returned to the couch with blankets, a pillow, and a pillowcase.

"Do you know Carol well?" Thia asked him, not moving from her position on the couch.

He set the linens down next to her and said, "No, only through mutual acquaintances. But in a small town like this, everyone knows everyone, even if they've never met."

Thia nodded.

After a moment, when Thia continued to sit, instead of lying down to sleep, Dr. Bachmann said, "I think I'll have some tea, too."

He put water on the stove to boil, and when his tea was ready, he returned to the living room to sit with her. They spoke infrequently, and when they did, it was Thia who would speak first. Dr. Bachmann would nod in response and help her work through her thoughts and memories so she could come to terms with what had to be done.

THE NEXT MORNING, THIA DROVE BACK TO Blairmont, having decided she would use the side door by the kitchen, go to the servants' quarters to pack her things, and leave. Then, she would go to her mother's house and stay with her, telling her simply that it was just not working out, as Dr. Bachmann had suggested.

Dr. Bachmann had offered to come with her, but she had told him it was not necessary. From what she understood— from all the hints Millie had given her about staying in the servants' quarters and from what she had read at the library with Dr. Manning—she would be okay as long as she did not enter the main part of the house, especially the south wing. And if she was confronted by Winifred, then she would tell her she was only there to grab some things and leave and that she would never return. Thia had nothing to fear, as long as she made it clear that Winifred was getting her way.

Going down that one-mile road from the town square to the entrance, Thia thought about the first time she had made that drive, how she had envisioned her guests making that same trip and thinking of what it would be like for them. The trees were, as she had imagined they would be that first day, bright and colorful on either side of her for as far as she could see. The blustery fall wind sent leaves flying into the air around her car, with not an ounce of humidity in the air, the cool breeze bringing the temperature down to jacket weather.

As she approached the entrance, she remembered that first time she looked through the iron columns at the house, how excited she had been to get inside it, how nervous Carol had been to step even one foot on the property.

And as she drove along the driveway, she looked at the gardens and the house, the ornate beauty that was almost too much to comprehend. She thought about the lake behind it, with the mountains in the distance, and she once again fell in love with Blairmont Manor and her dream of opening it to the public. She thought of her vision, of this being a place for people to visit, to hold events, and to vacation overnight. She thought of the garden parties, the weddings, the balls—and she found that she could not let it go. It was too perfect, too close to becoming a reality.

She recalled all the training sessions that she had taken in dealing with conflict resolution. They taught her to focus on finding common ground, to bestow the benefit of the doubt, and to first seek a compromise that would satisfy everyone before resorting to other means. She had learned negotiation tactics that would help people reach an agreement. She felt certain that she had the knowledge and experience to pull this off; previous owners had fled, but they did not have her education and background.

Instead of turning off the teardrop formation and parking under the porte cochere to access the side entrance next to the kitchen, she followed the driveway to park in front of the veranda, just as she had done that first day.

She walked up the stairs, crossed the veranda, and approached those two large wooden doors. Finding them locked, she rang the doorbell and asked, "Winifred? Can I come in?"

Everyone had told her to run away, to sell the place and leave. Dr. Manning had told her to get rid of Winifred, to force her to move on, either to another place on Earth or fully to the spiritual realm. Each person she had encountered had portrayed Winifred as a maniacal being. Not a single person had considered that Winifred could be anything other than pure evil.

But nobody was just plain evil. Thia could not accept that. Everyone had *something* good, about them or in them. And if what Dr. Manning had told her was true, then Winifred was just a girl in her late teens or early twenties who, for over a hundred years, had been treated as nothing other than an unwanted presence, a guilty criminal, and a poor servant who would not stay in her place.

"I don't like being summoned," Winifred said behind her.

Startled, Thia whipped around. *That smell,* she thought, fighting her gag reflexes.

"Are you here to gather your belongings so you can take them with you when you leave?" Winifred asked.

"Actually, I was hoping we could talk," Thia said.

Crossing her arms and raising an eyebrow, the ghostly form slowly lowered so that she appeared to be standing on the veranda.

"I understand why you want to stay here," Thia told her. "It's the most beautiful place I've ever been. But don't you want to move on? Is that why you are so mean to everyone, because you're frustrated that you're stuck here on Earth? I can help you move on to the spiritual realm."

"Would you be in a hurry to go to Hell?" Winifred asked her, expressionless.

"No, I suppose I would not," Thia said, wondering if that was an admission to the murder for which she had been accused when she was alive or if she was somehow going to be sent to Hell because of the things she had done after her death. "But there has to be a way to make this work."

"Make what work?" Winifred asked, anger creeping into her tone.

"You want to stay here, and so do I. And while I have been told I can make you leave, it's just not in my nature to do something like that. This house is huge. The property is enormous. Maybe I can run the hotel, and you can still stay here, but out of the way of the guests."

Winifred narrowed her eyes, and Thia took a step back, thinking of another compromise to propose.

But then Winifred's expression softened, and her form appeared to relax as her shoulders lowered and her arms loosened, her forearms now appearing to rest on each other as opposed to the tense grip they held previously. In a tone that was not at all harsh or defensive, a tone which Thia could not have imagined coming from this ghost, a tone that, dare Thia think, was possibly even kind and vulnerable, Winifred asked, "You want to live here with me?"

Thia nodded. "If we can make it work, yes I do. I don't want to force you out. But I also don't want to leave."

"Nobody's ever asked me to stay," Winifred said, her demeanor relaxing. "Nobody's ever asked me what *I* want."

Thia suppressed a smile but knew she could not hide her relief from her eyes. "Well, I'm asking," Thia said. She pulled out her phone and pulled up the picture Winifred had selected the previous day. Holding it up, she asked, "Are these your rules if we are to both stay here? Are these terms negotiable?"

"What do you have in mind?" Winifred asked.

Completely relaxed now, Thia smiled and said, "I know it will be an adjustment—for both of us—but I think we can come up with some kind of arrangement."

"Such as?"

Looking at the list on her phone, Thia said, "It says here that everyone should stay in the servants' quarters. But I want to have guests stay in the bedrooms, and I want to rent out the ballroom, the conservatory, and other rooms for special events. Eventually, I want to open a restaurant, with tables in the large dining hall, as well as in the back hall, the one with all the floor-to-ceiling windows with the view of the lake and the gardens. And I also want some rooms to be open for daily tours, for people who are interested in the history of the house." Then, the thought having just occurred to her, she added excitedly, "You could help me set that up! I bet you know loads of information about the original residents."

"And you would expect me to be…where?"

Thia shrugged. "I guess wherever you'd like, as long as it's out of the way. And, of course, I would prefer that you leave the guests alone." When Winifred did not respond, Thia asked, "Aren't you excited about it at all? You've been alone for all these years. Now you'll have people to watch, and it won't be so lonely like it has been."

"You are determined to make this happen, aren't you?" Winifred asked her.

"Yes, I am," Thia said. "But we can discuss the details. Maybe if you want certain rooms to remain untouched and blocked off, we can discuss that. And you can be in bedrooms when they're vacant. And of course you're free to roam the property."

"Am I?" Winifred asked sarcastically. "How kind of you."

Thia laughed and said, "Sorry, I'm trying to think of how we can come to a compromise. What are your thoughts? Shall we give it a shot and see how it goes? We'll make adjustments along the way, of course, as we learn what we can and cannot tolerate and live with…or *after*live, I guess it would be called, in your case."

Winifred held her gaze for a moment and then said, "In all my years"—Thia braced herself for another tongue-lashing—"nobody has ever suggested this."

With hope and excitement, Thia asked, "Do you think it will work?"

With a gleam in her eyes and a small smile, Winifred said, "We can certainly try."

Winifred slipped through the door, and Thia heard the deadbolt being unlocked, and then the door was opened. As for Winifred, she had vanished, but Thia crossed the threshold with a new outlook on this house, this "palace," as Monica had called it. Gretchen had been right—there was someone in the house, even if not a physical being like the one she had joked about. And that someone was Winifred, a girl who had been ignored, misunderstood, accused, and feared. But Thia had seen a different side of Winifred, a side no one else seemed willing to see, so quick were they to assume that the rumors and urban legends about her were true. Thia had been misjudged, too, many times in her life. Perhaps she and Winifred were not so different after all.

She thought about the past two months and how they had already been existing in that house together. In a way, it was almost comforting to her, to know someone else had been there the whole time. She had not been alone then. She was not alone now.

She went to her car to retrieve her notes and laptop and then went to the table in the kitchen to set up. She opened her laptop and took a deep breath. Over the past weeks, she had worked on everything to prepare for this moment, but thus far she had not pressed the submit buttons. Now, she went to each location and went live. She made her website visible and available to be found by search engines. She approved all of her advertising campaigns. And she made The Blairmont Manor Hotel available for booking on third party websites. Then, she went to a travel site and searched for a boutique hotel in the area, and there it was. Her hotel was listed right at the top, with a little white box saying "ad" in the corner of the picture—but hardly noticeable in her opinion, due to how stunning the mansion looked at sunset. The photographer had done a superb job. She clicked on the listing and viewed the photos and rooms available, unable to contain her joy and excitement.

Then, on a whim, she made the ballroom, lakeside hall, and gardens available to rent for private events. She had originally planned to gradually open all the services Blairmont Manor would offer, starting with booking overnight stays and then adding another service each month, until completion on Memorial Day the following year. But now she felt that a special occasion, from time to time, would not be too much for her to handle in addition to overnight guests.

She looked through her website once more to check it for accuracy and to make sure it was how she wanted it to be—but also to see it live, as if seeing it for the first time from the viewpoint of a prospective customer.

Feeling absolutely giddy, she got up and walked through the house, imagining guests and visitors. She walked along the great hall that had those beautiful, amazing two-story windows with the view of the gardens and the lake, the exquisite marble flooring, the marvelous sculptures in the alcoves of the opposite wall, those incredible chandeliers. She took the staircase to the second floor and walked to the front of the house, where the open hallway overlooked the grand entrance. As she descended the stairs, she imagined a bride also walking down those stairs, having dressed in one of the suites, her long train and veil flowing behind her, the photographer madly snapping hundreds of photos in succession as she made her way to the side gardens for the ceremony.

She envisioned tourists visiting for the day, having traveled from all over the world to see the historic home. She imagined them coming through those huge wooden doors for the first time, wearing fanny packs and walking shoes, their eyes and mouths widening with wonder at how impressed they were, feeling as though seeing this house was worth the drive.

She went to the sitting room to the right of the grand entrance hall. She had always hated how the three identical chairs were situated side by side along the wall.

"Winifred?" she asked into the air.

The ghost appeared in the room and said, "I told you I don't like to be summoned."

"Yes, I'm sorry," Thia said. "I'll remember that. See? This is good. We can tell each other little things like this, as they come up, to learn how we can best exist in the house together."

In her mind, she added getting potpourri and other ways to disguise the smell of Winifred to her ongoing to-do list.

"Anyway," Thia continued, "I would like to rearrange the furniture in this room so these three chairs are not next to each other, and maybe put two of them in different rooms so that each piece of furniture is different. On the list"—she pointed at her phone—"there's a rule to ask you prior to making any changes. May I summon you, then, when I would like to change something? Or maybe we can set a time and place to meet daily, if that's what you prefer."

Winifred softened and relaxed. She even smiled. "Thank you for consulting me first. Of course, you can change whatever you would like in the sitting rooms in this part of the house."

Feeling pleased, Thia grinned brightly and said, "Great. Thank you."

As she started to move the chairs around the room, Winifred disappeared, and Thia counted how long it took for that foul odor to dissipate.

"No, you can't do that," a hurried and anxious voice said

behind her. Millie had come to clean and immediately started moving the furniture back to where it had originally been.

"It's okay," Thia said reassuringly, placing a hand on Millie's shoulder. "She gave me permission to rearrange things in the sitting rooms."

Millie's eyes widened with horror. "Who?"

"I think you know," Thia said, "and I understand why you're afraid. But you don't need to be afraid anymore. She and I had a talk, and we've agreed to exist together in the house. She's okay with all the plans I have. I think she might even be excited, in her own way, to not be so alone anymore."

Millie said nothing but backed away and looked at Thia as though she had already failed, that same look she had always given Thia, that look of simultaneous apprehension and pity.

Ignoring it, Thia asked as she picked up an end table and moved it to another part of the room, "Are you going to the Halloween Festival in town today? I saw people decorating yesterday, and it looks like a lot of fun!"

Standing still and watching Thia, not offering to help, Millie replied, "Yes, I go every year."

Continuing to rearrange the furniture in the room, Thia said, "I was planning to go, too, and I wanted to because I really am trying to get to know everyone and become a part of the community. But then I was so busy the past two weeks that I didn't have time to get a costume or anything. And then I figured I should go anyway, until last night when I had a bit of a quarter-life crisis and was thinking of leaving Blairmont and this town. But now that everything is fine again, I think I will go."

Millie continued to watch her, standing now at the

entrance of the room, having slowly backed away while Thia had been talking and rearranging things.

"Does everyone dress up?" Thia asked. She had overheard some locals, when she was in town, talking about their costumes.

"Yes," Millie said curtly.

"Then I'll have to wear an old one," Thia said with a smile. She stopped moving and asked, "What will you be?"

"I need to get back to work," Millie said, and then she turned and left the room.

Thia sighed, but she was not discouraged. Despite having all her licenses and permits and being open for booking, she knew that between Winifred and Millie—and probably Herschel, too—she still had a lot of work to do in terms of relationship building. Millie would come around eventually. And if she did not, then Thia would, as Herschel had so eloquently put it, cross that bridge if she got to it.

As she continued on to the next sitting room, a sound from her phone alerted her to a notification. She checked it and gasped at what she saw. She ran to the kitchen, where her laptop was still on the table, checked the booking software she used for the hotel, and screamed when she saw it: someone had booked a room.

"Winifred!" she yelled, still looking at the screen. "Winifred!"

"What," the ghost said, irritated.

"I know you hate to be summoned, and I promise I won't do it for mundane, ordinary things, but *this—is—big*. Look!" She picked up the laptop and held it against her chest so that the screen was facing away from her and toward the ghost. "We got our first booking!"

Thia turned the laptop around so she could see the

screen, too, as she walked toward Winifred to show her more.

"It's a couple from up north. They booked the 'Sapphire Room' for a weekend next month!" Turning to Winifred, she said, "That's the one with that beautiful Spanish armoire. I named it the 'Sapphire Room' because of the canopy and stained-glass—"

"I've seen it," Winifred said, cutting her off.

"Yes, of course you know what I'm talking about."

Just then, Millie appeared in the doorway, having heard all the commotion.

"Millie, look!" Thia said to her excitedly.

But one look from Winifred, with a flash of anger in her eyes, sent Millie away. Thia heard her rush down the hallway next to the kitchen and exit through the side door.

Thia put the laptop back on the table and took a picture of the screen with her phone. Then, she sent the photo in a group text to her friends with the caption, "OFFICIALLY OPEN FOR BUSINESS!!!"—in all caps, with three exclamation points, a popping champagne emoji, and a GIF of someone dancing.

As she sent it, another notification popped up. This time, the "Emerald Room" had been booked for two nights in early December. "Another one!" she exclaimed to Winifred.

Completely beside herself now, Thia said, "I have to call my mom!"

As she called her mother and told her the news, Winifred disappeared, and various responses of congratulations came in from her friends, featuring GIFs and emojis of fireworks, toasts, and screaming for joy.

She spent the next hour in a state of sheer bliss, too distracted by the two bookings to do anything useful, but unable to stay still. She worked her way through the mansion, tidying up the rooms and making sure each one was exactly as she wanted it to be for her guests. The two bookings were weeks away, but for all she knew someone could book a room for a time even sooner. She made her way to the third floor of the south wing and heard awful music, with the worst sound quality her ears had ever been exposed to, coming from one of the bedrooms. As she followed the sound, she realized it was coming from the one she had named the "Ruby Room" because the lamps, though each different in uniqueness and design, had red pendants hanging from the lampshades and the sconces were encased in red glass.

When she entered, the bedroom was empty, and the lights were off. She crossed the large room, following the sound of the music, until she located it coming from the large sculpture of a woman in a garden. The gramophone was so well hidden within the design of the sculpture that Thia had not known it was there. The horn, she now saw, was disguised among the large flowers, and the base of the gramophone was hidden within the platform on which the sculpture sat. She looked behind the piece of art and saw a cabinet door above the hand crank. Being in a dark corner, she was not able to see clearly, so she activated the flashlight on her phone and used it to see how to open the small cabinet. Upon opening it, she could see the needle on the record. Setting her phone on the floor, she lifted the little arm with the needle, stopping the music, leaving only a small swishing sound as the record continued to spin.

Immediately, she felt herself being pulled back by her shoulders. Before she could comprehend what was happening, she found herself falling against the opposite wall in the servants' corridor between the bedrooms, hearing the sound of the door slamming shut behind her and the deadbolt turning so the door was locked. It was pitch-black, so dark she had to blink hard to convince herself her eyes were not closed.

She turned around and lifted her hands to shoulder level. With her back pressed against the wall behind her, she felt with her palms and fingers along the wall in front of her, where the door to the Ruby Room should have been, the passageway so narrow that she could not straighten her arms.

"Winifred?" she asked. "Millie?"

She felt part of the wall move, and heard the clicking sound as the servant door was caught by the deadbolt lock. She pressed harder and faster. *Click-click-click.*

"Winifred!" she yelled. "Winifred, open the door!"

Silence.

She looked around herself, unable to see, and turned around to face the wall behind her. She pressed along the wall with her fingertips, hoping to find the servant door to the bedroom next door.

She turned back around and started hitting the wall of the Ruby Room again as she yelled, "Millie? Winifred?"

She stopped hitting the wall and listened for a response.

Silence.

She felt her pockets for her phone, knowing she had set it on the floor next to the sculpture but hoping she had picked it up during all the commotion that had followed. But her pockets were empty. She felt the wall around her, hoping for a light switch. Having never been in the servants' passageways, she did not know where the light switch was— or if there even was one at all. She did not know how extensive the little hallways were between any of the rooms, let alone these two in particular. But she knew that somewhere there had to be access to a staircase or ladder that the servants had used in lieu of the main staircases.

She tried to remember the floor plans she and Monica's handyman had looked at together. She tried to remember that day in detail, trying to remember if the handyman had installed locks on *all* the servant doors and if she had gone around the house and actually locked *all* of them. She tried to remember if any were unlocked and if they were connected to these hidden passageways. As she thought through this idea of trying to find a way out, she became aware of the severity of the situation, how perilous it was for her to be stuck in this hidden network of dark and narrow tunnels, where Millie never went, in a house that nobody had any reason to enter. It might be days or weeks before anyone would find her—if anyone ever did.

Panicking, she began banging on the door with her fist and yelling.

Bang-bang-bang.

"Winifred!"

Bang-bang.

"Winifred, please! I'm sorry, I didn't know you were in there!"

Bang-bang-bang.

"You said we would figure this out together!"

Bang-bang-bang-bang-bang.

"Winifred, you promised!"

She stopped and listened.

Still, nothing but silence.

She tried again. She could not give up.

Bang-bang-bang.

"Winifred, please don't put me in this position! Don't make me have a professional come out here and exorcise you out of this house!"

Suddenly, the door swung open, and the narrow corridor was flooded with the dim afternoon light from the windows of the Ruby Room.

Thia ran past Winifred to the opposite side of the room, as far away from the servant door as she could get.

"I'm sorry," Winifred said. "I lost my temper. You said so yourself that this would take some getting used to."

Stunned by what had just happened, Thia did not respond at first.

"That's okay," she finally said in an exhale. "It's a learning process for both of us."

"It's getting late," Winifred said. "Don't you need to get ready for the festival? I heard you talking about it with Millie. You were so excited to go."

Thia stared at her for a moment, unable to think of anything other than what had just happened.

"Most of the festivities will be over by now," Winifred said, seemingly subdued, "but the adult party goes long through the night. You should go. It will give me some time to cool off and think about the house being full of overnight guests, what that will mean for me, and how I will need to change my habits."

"Yes," Thia agreed. "That's a good idea. It will give us both some time to cool off."

She left the room, retrieving her phone from the floor on her way out, still shocked by Winifred's reaction to her turning off the gramophone. She really had thought the room was empty. She had not seen—nor smelled—Winifred in there. She had not known Winifred was listening to that music, or whatever it was she was doing.

She went to her room in the servants' quarters and sat on her bed, considering all the advice she had been given by literally every person who would talk with her about Blairmont Manor. Each had suggested, either outright or through subtle hints, that she should sell it and start over somewhere else—or, as in Dr. Manning's case, try to get rid of Winifred.

Maybe this would not work.

In any case, she did want to get out of there. So she pulled an old costume out of her closet, one she had unpacked several weeks earlier as a backup, and got ready to leave.

As she crossed the entrance hall to the front doors, she heard Winifred say, "You could be my lady Mary Stinson in that dress."

Thia turned around and saw Winifred standing at the top of the stairs on the second floor.

"I'm Juliet," Thia said, "from Shakespeare's *Romeo and Juliet.*"

"She's still out there, you know," Winifred said, "in the lake. The kids in town used to say they could see her standing on the dock by the carriage house, especially on nights like this one, nights when the moon is full."

Thia laughed nervously at the thought.

"You had better get going. I'd hate for you to miss anything," Winifred said. "Have a good time."

"I will. Thanks."

Thia turned and left. As she descended the stairs of the veranda, a sheriff's deputy SUV pulled up and parked in front of her.

"Deputy Lawrence!" Thia said, greeting the deputy as

she stepped out of the vehicle. Thia looked for Deputy Carver through the windshield, but the passenger side was empty. "Alone?"

"Alone," Deputy Lawrence confirmed.

"What can I do for you?" Thia asked, having reached the driveway.

"Nothing, now that we've talked. I was sent here for a wellness check, and I can see that you are well."

"A wellness check?" Thia asked, surprised. "What on earth for?"

Deputy Lawrence checked her notes. "Millie called the Daffodil PD and said she was concerned about you. They called us, and here I am." She put her notes away. "On your way to the festival? Or are you headed to some swanky party in the city?"

"The festival. Are you going?"

"No, I'm on duty."

"Right," Thia said, seeing how that was obvious, "but you can stop by, right? I mean, as long as you don't have any other people to check on. Since I'll be *there*, you can at least be sure you won't have to come out here and clear the house again."

They both laughed.

"What are you supposed to be?" Deputy Lawrence asked.

"Juliet," Thia answered. "From *Romeo and Juliet*? It's an old costume. I went as a couple with my ex a few years back. I know it's lame, but I didn't have anything else to wear."

"Yeah, you might want to add some fake blood and gore. She killed herself, right?"

"Yes, I suppose she did. I guess I'm dressed as the character before she died."

"It's okay. People will cut you some slack since it's your

first time, but you won't be winning 'best costume' in that."
Deputy Lawrence started walking back to her SUV. "We
tend to go all out at these things. You'll see. Not only with
Halloween, but with every holiday."

"Really? That's perfect!" Thia said. "This really is my
kind of town."

"Need a ride?" Deputy Lawrence asked.

"Um…" Thia considered the offer, but then, curious, she
glanced toward the carriage house. "Actually, I have one
more thing to do before I go. But maybe I'll see you there."

"All right," Deputy Lawrence said. "I'll see you around."

Deputy Lawrence drove off, and Thia walked along the
driveway, through the porte cochere, and followed it to the
carriage house. She looked at the lake, wondering if the "kids
in town," as Winifred had said, were telling the truth. Since
moving to Blairmont, she had been warned by various locals
that kids would trespass on the property. No one had said it
was haunted back then, but now she knew why the kids
dared each other to come here. She remembered an old,
abandoned house near her childhood home, where she and
other kids from the neighborhood would play and tell stories
to scare each other. The difference was that she had not
believed in ghosts back then.

But if Winifred could be in the house, then Mary Stinson
could be in the lake.

She stepped off the driveway and onto the grass and
went out onto the dock. The sun had set behind the hills, the
twilight having turned the trees around her into two-
dimensional shadows before they disappeared into the cool
night. The full moon was already high, and sparse clouds,
long and thin, hung in the dark blue sky, where only the
brightest of stars were yet visible.

Suddenly, Thia felt foolish. What had she expected? To see Mary Stinson and talk to her as she had with Winifred? She laughed softly to herself and turned to leave.

"It's beautiful out here, isn't it?" Winifred asked, appearing next to Thia.

By now, Thia was used to Winifred's appearance and was no longer shocked or scared by it. It was not Winifred's fault she looked as menacing as she did. It was not like Winifred could do anything about it. The smell, however, was one that would take a bit longer to get over. At least with the outside air, it was not as pungent.

Thia replied, "I don't think I could ever get tired of this view."

"I don't like when humans trample on the grass around the house," Winifred scolded her.

Thia sighed. "Yes, I'm sorry, but there's hardly a path to the dock, is there? I'll have one built so that no one walks on the grass here." She would wait until later to tell Winifred she planned on letting the guests roam the property as much as they desired. One thing at a time.

"That would work," Winifred said pleasantly.

Thia turned back to face the water and smiled, feeling warm satisfaction fill her heart. It had not been easy; there had been unexpected setbacks; and she knew she still had some hurdles to get over. But she had rooms booked at her hotel, and she had resolved her first conflict as a business owner. There was no conspiracy by the townspeople to get her to leave, no psychological condition causing hallucinations or delusional thinking. Only a misjudged presence in the house, which she had managed to win over with kindness and an open mind.

Standing there together, as friends and partners, they watched the water turn black and the stars come out as the last light of day was overcome by night.

12

WHEN THIA OPENED HER EYES, WINIFRED'S FACE was inches from her own. Upon seeing Winifred, she screamed and sat up.

"I'm sorry for screaming. I just didn't expect to see your face like that when I woke up."

Thia looked around herself, recognizing that she was in one of the bedrooms on the third floor, the one she had named the "Scarlet Room" for its scarlet wallpaper, with velvet flowers that were slightly darker than the cloth background.

"I didn't expect you to wake up at all," Winifred said, amused. "But here you are, awake!"

"Look, I know we said it would take some getting used to, existing together in this house, but I would appreciate it if in the future you did not…"—Thia flicked her hand in the air where she had been lying—"do that."

"It's not like I've been watching you all along," Winifred said, still utterly amused, nearly manic in her delight. "It's not like I knew you were going to wake up at that exact moment. It's not like you've ever woken up before when I was that close."

It was then that Thia realized the smell was gone, for she

was certain it would have woken her up with Winifred that close to her nose. She hoped it was not because she had become used to it already. She would hate for her guests to have to endure such a rotten odor because she could no longer notice it.

She started to slide off the bed, only to discover she was not sliding. She was floating.

Winifred continued excitedly, "I can't believe you woke up. Truly, I was not sure you ever would. But I was so fascinated by you being here I couldn't tear myself away. This has never happened before! No one has ever stuck around like this. I haven't even bothered to play with the Morrisons. That's how distracted I've been by you being here."

"I don't remember sleeping in this room," Thia said, looking around. She looked down at herself. She was still wearing her Juliet costume.

"I have no idea why you're here—here in the house or here in this room," said Winifred. "I was just wandering in the hallway, playing, when I went by the door, and here you were! At first I was here all the time, waiting to see if anything would happen. Then, I left, figuring you would lie here forever. But then I came back because I was so curious. And no matter how much noise I made or how much I poked at you or tried to wake you, you just lay there, still and silent, like a carcass on the side of the road."

Thia stared at her, having no idea what she was talking about.

Winifred continued, "Like I said, I've been so fascinated by your presence I haven't even begun with the Morrisons. I've seen them, of course, a couple of times. They've only come here a few weekends."

"Who are the Morrisons?" Thia asked, completely confused.

"The new owners," Winifred said, as though Thia should have already known.

Thia furrowed her brow, now more confused than before.

Winifred continued, "We have *so much* work to do. They've moved *everything*. I'm certain Millie tried to stop them, but I'm pretty sure they got rid of a few things, so we'll have to track them down. If she was smart about it, Millie convinced them to let her handle it so she could store them in the carriage house."

Winifred glided toward the door. Then, when she realized Thia was not following her, she turned around and said, "Come on! There's fun to be had. The Morrisons just arrived for the weekend."

Thia got up to walk across the room, but she was not walking. Like Winifred, she was *gliding*.

"Winifred," Thia said, grasping what was happening, "why are the Morrisons the owners of Blairmont Manor now?"

Winifred turned around and said to her, again as though Thia should have already known this, "Because your mother sold it to them after you died."

"*Died?*" Thia repeated. "I'm *dead?*"

Panicking, she looked down at herself again, her form levitating above the floor. She was not breathing. She *could not* breathe, even as she felt like she was hyperventilating.

"What happened?" she asked. "How did I die?"

But Winifred had already disappeared into the hallway.

Thia tried to lower herself as she had seen Winifred do on the veranda. She watched as her heels lowered to the floor. She could not feel it. Then, her feet disappeared beneath the floorboards.

Reappearing in the doorway, Winifred said impatiently, "*Come on.*"

"How do I get back up?" Thia asked.

Winifred made a noise of frustration and floated down the corridor toward the stairs.

"Wait!" Thia yelled after her. "Wait! What happened? How did I die? Why am I here?"

As she thought of following Winifred, her form rose above the floor and floated toward the hallway. She followed Winifred down the hall, calling after her, "What happened to me? I don't remember anything!"

Winifred stopped and turned around, annoyed. "You drowned in the lake. Millie saw your body floating in the water through one of the windows on the third floor. She called the authorities. They took your body away. And then one day, like I said, I was just walking by, minding my own business, and there you were, lying in that bed." She turned around and continued down the hall.

"How could that happen? I know how to swim, and that lake is not that deep."

When Winifred did not answer, Thia rushed after her. "What about my mom? You said she sold Blairmont Manor. When did all this happen?"

"Months ago," Winifred said as she descended the stairs, not bothering to turn around.

"*Months?* What is today's date? Where is my mom now? Is she okay?"

Winifred ignored her, having turned to go down the second flight of stairs. From where they were on the staircase, Thia could see a door on the first floor that led outside. She thought of going to it, and her form floated through the stairs in a direct path to the door. Out of habit, she tried to open it, but her hand slid right through the handle. She thought of being on the other side of it, and her form went through the door.

Having the hang of it now, she floated as fast as she could along the driveway. She tried to simply imagine *being* at her mother's house, figuring that if thinking of floating toward the door had led her there, then perhaps thinking of being somewhere specific would transport her to that location. But apparently that was not how it worked. Speeding up, she glided along the driveway, heading straight to the gate, which had been reattached. She would glide all the way to her mother's house if she had to.

But upon reaching the gate, she was knocked back. She tried to go forward again, but again she was shoved back by an invisible force. She tried again, and again it did not work. She went along the fence, feeling with her hands, trying to find a break in the force field, but she was continually met with a repulsion that felt like trying to force the same pole of two magnets to touch.

She turned and floated back to the house, where Winifred was outside a room, looking in and watching the living humans.

Without paying any attention to them, Thia asked her, "How do I leave the property?"

Looking at Thia as though she were some kind of moron, Winifred replied, "You just *do*."

"I tried," Thia said. "I can't get past the fence."

"Just go *through* it," Winifred said.

"I *can't*," Thia told her.

Winifred made a noise of frustration and started floating toward the door.

They left together, Thia trailing Winifred, who was much faster than she was. When they reached the gate, Winifred continued on, but Thia was stuck on the property.

Winifred turned around to look at her. "Just keep going," she said.

"I *can't*," Thia told her again. "How did you do it?"

Winifred said, "I just *did*."

Winifred watched in amusement as Thia tried several more times to cross over the property line. "Interesting," she said finally. But then she quickly became bored and said, "Well, it looks like you have some work cut out for you," and went back to the house.

Thia floated all along the fence until she came to the end of it. Then she tried to go around it, without success. She continued on another hundred yards, feeling that same repulsive force all along the way. She floated up to the treetops and tried crossing there, but even then, she could not. Eventually, she gave up and went back to the house.

On her way, she saw Herschel in the side garden.

"Herschel!" she called to him and sped up to greet him.

Some of the flowers and bushes looked as though they were getting ready to bud. He was tending to them, trimming back dead parts of the plants and pulling out new weeds that had sprung up with the promise of warm weather to come.

"Herschel!" she yelled again, right next to him now.

He continued his work without the slightest indication he knew she was there. She tried to touch him, to tap him on the shoulder, but her finger went right through him. She tried a couple more times before realizing it was no use. She needed answers and guidance. She needed to be taught how to exist in this ghostly form.

She went back to the house in search of Winifred and found her in the sitting room, observing the living humans. When she appeared in the doorway, Winifred held her finger to her lips, signaling for Thia to be quiet.

"It doesn't matter," Thia said. "Nobody can see or hear me."

A flash of anger crossed Winifred's eyes, and in an instant she had floated over to be next to Thia. In a harsh whisper, she admonished her, "Don't *ever* do that again."

"Do what?" Thia asked.

"First and foremost, disobey me. But also don't just talk or do anything to make your presence known, not until you know if the humans can sense you."

"Okay," Thia whispered. "Why not?"

"Because this is my house and I was here first. If you are to stay here, you do as *I* say."

"So I can never talk around the humans unless you give me permission?" Thia asked.

"Some are more receptive to us than others. Remember, it took you a *long* time to finally be open to my existence. You have to figure out who is most open and who is most closed. Then, from there you can start planning your strategy."

"Strategy for what?" Thia asked.

The four humans were sitting, chatting and laughing, two on a sofa and two in chairs, which they had moved to be closer to the sofa.

"Those two," Winifred said, pointing to the ones in the chairs, "are the Morrisons, the new owners. The other two are their friends. They're staying here for the weekend."

Winifred lowered herself and walked around the humans, circling them slowly. Thia tried to follow her but ended up gliding instead.

"They don't hear us," Winifred said. "You lucked out this time."

One of the humans stood up and went to a table that was against a wall. A bottle of bourbon sat on top of it, with four crystal glasses Thia recognized as having been part of a set from a curio in another room. He poured them each a glass and handed one to each of the other humans.

"You see," Winifred began instructing, continuing to walk in a circle around the group, "each human is different, but not only different in susceptibility and being able to sense us. Each human has different fears, different tolerances, and different limits in terms of what they can handle. They are each different, even if only slightly, in what will scare them and how far it can go before they can no longer continue to live in denial."

She stopped, so Thia stopped, too.

"How do I walk, like you're doing?" Thia asked. She tried to stand on the floor, but, like the last time she had tried, she sank through it.

"Hush," Winifred responded. She was listening to the conversation. Then, she said, "Listen so you can learn about them. Find out what their fears and desires are so you can form a strategy."

"Strategy for what?" Thia asked again.

Ignoring her question, Winifred continued, "It doesn't always matter what they want. But sometimes it can make things more interesting and more fun. These new owners seem pretty boring, but it sounds like they plan to spend the summer here and have friends over often. I don't know if I want to deal with having so many humans in the house this summer, though, so we'll get rid of them before then." She turned to look at Thia and said, "That's another part of the strategy: timing. You have to decide when you want things done and how long you want these people here. A weekend every now and then is no big deal, but to be here all the time, especially with other guests—no I don't want that." Then, she corrected herself. "*We* don't want that, do we?"

"Why not?" Thia asked.

Again ignoring her, Winifred said, "So the key is to try little things at first and slowly figure them out. We already know they can't see or hear us, but let's see how they react to what they *can* see and hear."

In an instant, she was next to the fireplace. She knocked a silver candlestick off the mantle.

Upon hearing it hit the floor, the four humans turned to see what had caused the noise.

"Did you see that?" one of the Morrisons asked.

Winifred began to snicker and put her hand over her mouth to stop herself from laughing.

"No, what happened?" one of the friends asked, having had her back to the fireplace.

"That candlestick just fell off the mantle," the Morrison human said, "all by itself."

Even though she was covering her mouth to suppress it, Thia could hear Winifred chuckling, a sound she now recognized from the time she had been sitting at the desk when the drawer had slowly slid out.

The other friend went to that part of the room, and Winifred moved out of the way so as not to be touched. Picking it up, he said, "It's too heavy to just fall over like that."

"That's odd," the first friend said.

Winifred chuckled again, watching the scene unfold.

"Maybe it's the ghost of Cynthia Watkins," one of the Morrisons said jokingly.

Winifred lowered her hand to her chin and looked at Thia, her eyebrows raised, her eyes wide, and her grin filled with delighted amusement as she mouthed, "*That's you!*"

"Who is that?" one of the friends asked.

The other Morrison responded, "The previous owner. She killed herself."

The two friends—as well as Thia—gasped.

"I know it's strange, and please don't tell anyone," the first Morrison said. "And please don't judge us for buying the estate after finding that out. It was a steal! We couldn't pass it up."

"After much, *much* nagging," the other Morrison continued, "the realtor finally told us the story and why the price was so low. The girl was in her twenties, living here all alone."

"Oh my," one of the friends said. "She sounds like she was troubled."

Thia's eyes widened in disbelief. "No!" she screamed. "I wasn't *troubled*. I was building a business! I was successful! I had bookings and contracts and permits and licenses!"

"So when she committed suicide," the first Morrison continued, "her mother was apparently very distraught and just wanted to get rid of this property as fast as she could. She even left all this furniture." With a wave of an arm to indicate their surroundings, the first Morrison added, "She left *everything*."

"Even these," the other Morrison said, holding up one of the crystal glasses.

"Wow," one of the friends said.

The humans continued talking, but Thia ignored them,

crossing the room and asking, "Winifred, why do they think I killed myself?"

Winifred responded nonchalantly. "I may have staged it that way. It's a much faster process·to get through than any other way to die, fewer cops and investigators and forensic teams and such."

"So you got the coroner to rule it as a suicide? How?" Thia asked. "There's no way my mom or my friends would believe that. I'm sure they demanded an investigation."

"There was no need. It was undeniable. Your toxicology results showed you had consumed more than enough to die, and the empty prescription bottle on the dock was all they needed to match what was in your body with what pills you had swallowed and where you got them."

"What are you talking about?" Thia asked, still in disbelief. "What prescription? What drugs? I didn't take anything that day, let alone a whole bottle of pills."

"Yes, you did. You swallowed a whole bottle of sleeping pills and then jumped into the lake." Winifred had been suppressing a smile, but now she could no longer contain it, so proud of herself was she.

"No, I didn't," Thia declared forcefully.

"Okay, *you* didn't," Winifred conceded. "I possessed your body, swallowed all the pills in the bottle, jumped into the lake, and then when you were dead, I returned to the house."

"What pills?" Thia asked. "I didn't have a prescription for sleeping pills."

"I took the bottle from the lockbox at Dr. Bachmann's house," Winifred confessed. "The one from which he got a pill for you the night I literally threw you out of the house— I had to. You wouldn't leave!"

"Oh no," Thia whispered to herself, seeing how Winifred

had staged it. She had told Dr. Bachmann that morning there was no need for him to accompany her when she returned to Blairmont. She had told him she was going to pack her things and leave. Could he possibly think she would have stolen a bottle of pills and killed herself instead? If he believed that, Thia could only imagine the guilt he felt.

"He lost his license, of course," Winifred continued. "About time. The fool should never have been allowed to practice medicine anyway. Psychiatrists aren't *real* doctors."

Thia backed away from her. "I can't believe you did that."

"Look, the humans are over it and are talking about something else," Winifred said, having moved on. "Pick something up and throw it. I want to see if it scares them."

Thia did not move but simply continued to stare with disgust at this hideous being who had murdered her.

Winifred asked, "Isn't this what you wanted? To coexist with me?"

"No!" Thia replied. "I wanted to *live*—as a live human being—in this house, and I wanted peaceful relations, and I wanted to be a good hostess, and I didn't want to have any conflict, and I didn't want to have to be in a situation where I would have to kick someone out! It wasn't *you* I wanted, it was the house!"

Angry now, Winifred moved so she was behind one of the chairs the Morrisons were sitting in. Still holding Thia's gaze, she lifted the chair, forcing the human sitting in it to fall face-forward onto the floor.

The other three humans screamed and stood up, staring at the chair now suspended in the air, presumably on its own because they could not see Winifred holding it.

"Help me move these things back to where they belong," Winifred commanded Thia.

As Winifred returned the chair to its original position against the wall, the three other humans helped the one who had fallen to the floor and then scurried out of the room.

Winifred slid the other chair back to where she wanted it to be.

Thia crossed the room and began to leave.

"Where are you going?" Winifred asked her. "You have to help me."

"I can't," Thia said, backing out of the room and into the grand entrance hall. "I just can't."

She continued floating backward until she turned around to float forward, not having any plan of where she was going or what she was doing. She needed to process everything that was going on, to try to comprehend, even if only a tiny bit, this nightmare she was now in.

She thought of her friends and family and what they must have endured the past few months. She thought about how thinking she had killed herself would affect them for the rest of their lives. They would not only have to deal with mourning the loss of her life but also with wondering if they had missed something, wondering if there had been anything they could have done to prevent it from happening. She imagined them going through memories, over and over again, searching for any signs they should have seen but did not, thinking of things they should have said or done differently—all for naught because she had not actually killed herself, but they would never know it. With the way Winifred had staged her death, nobody would ever know she was murdered.

What was worse was that she had no means to physically purge the emotions she felt. As a non-physical being, she could not cry. She tried to sob, but it was only noise without tears, leaving her feeling empty.

She wandered the halls and looked again at all the ornate woodwork on the walls and ceilings, the enormous chandeliers, the porcelain and marble sculptures, the clocks, the windows, the incredible art that lined the walls—how different it was to be on this side of it. Her beautiful hotel, still here, but without her.

All the changes she had made were restored back to the way they had been when she had first moved in. All the swing bar locks and deadbolt locks were gone, the drill holes having been filled and covered. There was not a single security camera on the premises. The gate had been recovered and reattached. All the outdoor furniture she had purchased was gone. All her new linens were nowhere to be found. Aside from the new mattresses and the Victorian-style lamplights at the entrance, which Winifred had apparently decided to keep, there was no evidence Thia had ever lived there.

She thought of all her visions for the hotel, all the parties and balls, all the guests from around the world, all the interesting people she would meet. She had envisioned an orchard or a vineyard and one day building a cottage for herself somewhere on the property. She had thought she would live here the rest of her life, long into old age.

All of it was still here, but now out of her reach.

When she reached the ballroom, she could barely look at it. Weddings, anniversary parties, debutante balls and quinceañeras, maybe business conferences and fundraisers— all of these, she had imagined happening in this space. She had wanted to provide a beautiful location for these celebrations. She had wanted to help make a special day perfect for someone—for many people. She had envisioned that over her lifetime, she would see hundreds of celebrations in this room—this room that was now dark and empty, in a house owned by a couple that planned on using it only for the summer and on the occasional weekend. What a waste.

Suddenly, the sconces that lined the walls came on, and Winifred said behind her, "Stop moping around. It's depressing."

She went past Thia into the ballroom, holding her arms out as if she had a partner, and started waltzing and humming. "I danced with him once, you know. Did I ever tell you that?"

"With the heir to Blairmont?" Thia guessed.

"No, no, no, of course not. I don't know if he even knew I existed, the fool." She continued on, circling until she was in the center of the ballroom. "Mr. Stinson, my employer. He came home very late one night. The butler was out— somehow he got the night off, family emergency or something—and none of the other servants were awake. I don't remember why I was still awake. But when I heard him come in, I offered to take his coat and hat since no one else was there. He was in such a jolly mood. He took me in his arms and sang while he danced with me in the entryway, just like this, until he reached the stairs. And then he went up to his bed, still wearing his coat and hat and everything." She hummed some more, and Thia recognized it as the same song that had been playing on the gramophone when Winifred had shoved her into the servants' hallway. "He was very drunk, I'm sure," Winifred continued, "but we danced."

Thia backed out of the room and continued roaming the halls. By dawn, she had made her way to the kitchen, where one of the friends was getting a glass of water, wearing workout clothes and running shoes, having presumably just returned from a morning run.

The other friend came in, still wearing pajamas. "You couldn't sleep either?" he asked.

With her mouth full of water, the runner shook her head. After swallowing, she said, "I can't get over what happened last night."

"Yeah, that totally freaked me out," he said, going to the refrigerator.

Thia looked at the refrigerator and saw that it was new. It occurred to her, then, just how odd and random these updates were that Winifred permitted. Perhaps, as the rules suggested, she truly did not care about the servants' quarters because she rarely went to them, not now that she considered herself the mistress of the house and no longer a servant.

The two friends went to the kitchen table and sat. As they were talking, Thia saw a fork on the counter and, out of habit, picked it up to put it in the sink. But just before setting it down, she lifted it up again and held it close to her face, realizing she had *picked it up.* Her hand did not go through it as it had with everything else. She could *feel* it in her hand, not as a solid object, but as a repelling force, like what she felt at the boundary of the property but on a much smaller scale.

"Throw it at them," Winifred said behind her. Thia turned around to look at her. "They don't see it." The two friends were sitting with their backs to Thia.

But instead, Thia marveled at being able to pick up a physical object and hold it. She did not know how she was doing it.

With a huff of frustration, Winifred said again, "*Throw it.*"

Too distracted, however, Thia ignored her command and instead asked, "How is this possible?"

Winifred crossed the room and pulled a kitchen knife out of the block on the counter. "Like this," she said and threw the knife toward the table.

Both of the humans, as well as Thia, screamed. The humans stood up and turned around, looking right at Winifred but not seeing her.

"What just happened?" the runner asked, while Thia screamed at Winifred, "*Why did you do that?*"

Winifred picked up another knife and waved it in the air. "Like this, see? Do this."

The humans' faces went pale as they watched the knife wave in the air and then slowly levitate toward them.

"*What are you doing?*" Thia exclaimed, full of fear for them, knowing, firsthand, that Winifred was capable of murder.

Winifred was giggling as she inched closer and closer to the humans. Thia, stunned and unable to move for fear and disbelief, could only watch as Winifred started thrashing the knife in the air more rapidly with larger swings. Then, she glanced at Thia and, as though showing off, slashed one of the humans across the arm. The other human grabbed a towel and held it to the gash, the towel instantly soaking with blood.

While Thia was paralyzed with terror, Winifred just laughed and laughed, unable to control herself.

The two humans quickly ran out of the room, yelling toward the rest of the house to warn the Morrisons as they left for the hospital.

Winifred dropped the bloody knife, and it fell onto the floor, clanking against the tile several times before finally settling. Victoriously, she said, "That didn't last as long as I would have preferred, but I dare say the Morrisons won't be coming back after their friends tell them about this."

Thia looked back at her, too terrified to speak.

"Don't worry," Winifred said as she left the room, "someone new to play with will come along eventually."

BUT THE MORRISONS DID COME BACK. OVER THE next two weeks, Winifred had Millie track down all the missing furniture, artwork, and books that had been sold, and she put everything back to the way it had been when Thia first saw the house. Thia tried, multiple times, to be seen or heard by Millie or Herschel, and she tried to break through the force field along the property lines, all to no avail.

And then one day, Thia heard a car in the driveway. She rushed to the nearest window, Winifred showing up next to her only a moment later.

"That was fast," Winifred said.

But there was only one car, and Carol was nowhere to be seen. Thia and Winifred watched as the Morrisons got out of the car, followed by a woman getting out of the back seat.

"Oh, for heaven's sake, they didn't," Winifred said.

"Didn't what?" Thia asked. "Who is that?"

"It's one of those paranormal weirdos. I've never met this one, but they're all the same. They all come in here, all smug and arrogant, thinking they can get rid of me, just like that."

"Weirdos?" Thia asked.

"It's a word I learned from a kid who lived here a couple decades ago," Winifred responded, as if Thia had been surprised by Winifred using the word.

"No, I know you keep yourself updated on some things"—Thia glanced around the room—"but not others. I meant, how can you be skeptical of paranormal professionals when you are a ghost?"

"I'm skeptical of her so-called powers. Nobody can get rid of me."

"But what about me?" Thia asked hopefully, looking out the window. When Winifred did not respond, Thia turned around and saw that the room was empty.

Thia followed Winifred to the part of the second floor that overlooked the grand hall at the front of the house. As the humans entered, the spiritualist immediately looked up and around the large entry hall, but she did not see the ghosts.

"It happened in here," one of the Morrisons said, guiding the medium to the sitting room where Winifred had forced one of them out of the chair.

Winifred chuckled. "Get ready," she said. "This will be fun."

"You've been through this before?" Thia asked. "What's going to happen?"

"Come," Winifred commanded. "We'll scare her in the dining hall. I know where there's some rope we can use to hang ourselves. Then, when she explores the house, she'll find us."

"What if I don't want to do that?" Thia asked Winifred as she floated away.

Winifred whipped around with anger. "You will do as *I* say. You are in *my* house." Then, she turned and went away.

Unsure of what to do, Thia remained where she was. A few minutes later, she was in the sitting room with the humans, not knowing how she had gotten there.

"Cynthia Watkins?" the medium asked in a way that indicated it was not the first time she said the name. Thia recalled Winifred telling her she did not like being summoned and reasoned that must have been what had happened to her, how she had seemingly teleported from her position on the second floor to now being in this room. The woman and the Morrisons were sitting on the floor in the center of the room, having moved all the furniture out of the way, circled around some candles and holding hands.

"If you are here," the medium continued, "knock three times."

Boom.

Thia turned toward the noise to see Winifred in the entryway next to one of the large wooden doors. She hit it again with her fist. *Boom.*

Expecting a third, Thia watched her, but she only giggled, meeting Thia's eyes with a mischievous grin.

Thia turned back to the room where the humans were. They were equally puzzled, also waiting for that third knock.

"Why were there only two?" one of the Morrisons asked.

The spiritualist asked, "Is there someone else in this house? If so, knock three times."

Boom, Winifred again made the noise. Then another. *Boom.*

But no third.

Thia looked at her, bemused, but again Winifred only giggled.

Thia went to a side table nearby and tried to beat her fist on the top of it as Winifred had knocked on the door, intending to do it three times to let them know she was there. But she was unable to produce any sound.

Winifred, floating next to her, started laughing loudly. "Come on," she said. "She'll start looking for us in the rest of the house. Let's give her a show."

Winifred left, but instead of following her, Thia moved to be next to the humans, determined to make contact. She tried to tap the shoulder of the clairvoyant woman, as Winifred had touched her shoulder in the deputy's car that night of the bells. But just as it had when she tried to touch Herschel, her finger went through the woman's shoulder.

But unlike the time she tried to tap Herschel's shoulder, this time she found herself sitting on the floor, in the circle, each of her hands holding a hand of one of the Morrisons.

"Hello?" she asked, and the Morrisons opened their eyes and looked at her. Based on the way they looked at her, she realized she was *inside* the medium. She took a deep breath. She could feel air enter the lungs! "Please," she pleaded, "when she returns to this body, please ask her how I can move on, how I can get out of this house and be fully in the spiritual realm. Or how I can at least get beyond the gate. I have to—"

Suddenly, she was thrust out of the medium's body and was floating next to her.

The medium immediately blew out the candles and started gathering her things as she said with urgency, "We have to leave. Now."

"What happened?" one of the Morrisons asked.

"There are two spirits in this house. One is so sinister it is beyond what my powers can handle. The other one is trapped here by the evil one."

The medium ushered the Morrisons ahead of her to the

front doors.

Trapped, Thia thought. *No, that can't be!*

She followed them across the veranda, down the stairs, and into the car. She touched the medium, and Thia again found herself inside the woman's body as the car sped off down the driveway.

"Please!" she implored them. "My name is Thia Watkins, and I'm trapped here. Please, tell this woman she has to help me get out of here. Or if she can't do that, please ask if she could check on my mom and my friends and then come back here to tell me how they're doing. I just want to know they're okay. I can't—"

She felt a jolt as she was forced out of the woman's body and out of the car as it passed through the entrance and drove down the road toward the town square.

Remaining at the edge of the property, full of despair, Thia watched as the car got smaller in the distance.

All she could think about was that awful word: *trapped*.

"That was enlightening," Winifred said. Then, she made a show of crossing the property line and started to float backward, still facing Thia as she headed toward the town square.

"Where are you going?" Thia asked.

"I want to make sure they don't come back."

"How?" Thia asked her. "Winifred, what are you going to do?"

But Winifred only laughed as she held Thia's gaze and continued to float backward, through trees and bushes, speeding up to catch up with the Morrisons and their spiritualist.

13

JUST AS WINIFRED HAD PROMISED, ANOTHER FAMILY came to replace the Morrisons. Thia watched as Carol showed the property. All the showings were short, for Carol was quite proficient when it came to inventing excuses to get people to leave. Several came only to see it out of curiosity. Others came with serious intentions of buying, only to think that it was too much to take on. They wanted something more manageable, simpler, less extravagant.

The Choos, however, were from a big city up north, and they wanted to raise their kids in a small town, in a community that lacked the pressure and stress that came with city life. Thia was able to learn all of this because, like when she met Thia, Carol stalled before opening the gate, hoping to deter potential buyers from even considering going inside Blairmont Manor.

Thia and Winifred were just inside the gate, watching Carol and the Choos standing on the other side, unaware of the ghosts observing them. Thia could not help but recall when she first saw Blairmont, how she had stood at the gate alone, making notes in her notebook and plans in her mind. How she was, like the Choos were now, totally unaware of Winifred watching.

"She's cute, isn't she?" Winifred asked.

"Who?" Thia asked.

"Carol. She's the only one I'll allow to show the property."

"Why?"

Winifred did not answer at first, but then she said, "She's the most entertaining."

You mean the most scared, Thia thought.

"She hates coming here," Winifred continued. "Sometimes I count how long it takes her to finally go inside." Winifred laughed.

Thia remembered how Carol kept saying, "*If* you decide to buy," and how Carol had documents about the house that a realtor would have been obligated to share with potential buyers but did not until Thia put a formal offer on the house. At the time, she thought Carol did not think she was a serious potential buyer, assuming she was too young or too poor. Now, she knew better. Now, she knew it was because Carol was not trying to sell her the house at all; rather, she was trying to dissuade her from it.

"I hope they buy it," Winifred whispered.

"I thought you wanted the house to be empty," Thia argued.

"I do, but if anyone is going to move in, I hope it's these people."

"Why?" Thia asked.

Winifred looked at her, annoyed. "Aren't you paying any attention at all? They just said they have kids. Young kids."

Thia dared to ask, "And that's good because…?"

"I love when kids move in. Their parents never believe them. They tell their kids that what they see and hear is not real, that it's only their imagination, and in doing so they teach their children not to trust their own senses. The psychological trauma lasts a lifetime, not to mention it destroys any trust and safe feelings the kids have in themselves, their parents—and really anyone—for the rest of their lives. But"—and this was when Winifred got really excited—"the real reason I love when kids move in is because there's nothing better than the look on a parent's face when they realize they should have listened to their children, that beautiful mixture of simultaneous disbelief and guilt. I can't wait for you to see it. It's a glorious moment, when they realize that the bond and all the trust they've developed over the child's short life so far is completely shattered."

Horrified by what she was hearing, Thia whispered, more to herself than to Winifred, "You're a monster!"

"And so, too, are you now," Winifred countered.

"I am nothing like you."

"You will be soon enough."

"You mean you weren't always like this?" Thia did not know if the thought terrified her, thinking she could turn into Winifred, or if the thought gave her hope, thinking if Winifred had not always been like this then maybe there was the possibility she could return to being good.

Winifred thought for a minute. Then, she finally said, "Good point. I suppose I have always been like this." Then, changing her mood, she said, "This will be a fun experiment, won't it? To see if you become this way, too, now that you're a ghost, like me."

With strong conviction, Thia declared, "I will never be like you."

Winifred ignored Thia and continued observing the Choos so she could strategize the best way to terrorize her next victims.

A MONTH LATER, THE CHOOS MOVED IN. WINIFRED'S excitement was palpable.

"We'll leave the parents alone," she told Thia as they watched the family marvel at the house, unexpectedly completely furnished. "We'll only reveal ourselves to the children."

"Why can't we just coexist?" Thia asked. "This house is big enough for the six of us. We can easily stay out of their way."

Furious, Winifred said, "Because this is *my* house and no one else's. *You're* not even supposed to be here."

"Then why did you kill me and trap me here?" Thia asked.

"Do you really think you're the first person I've killed? In this house, even?" Winifred laughed. "No, I assure you, not at all. You're just the first fool to stick around. Why don't *you* leave?"

"I *can't*," Thia said. "Believe me, I want to."

They continued to watch the Choo family. Winifred began scheming, coming up with the perfect plan, first to scare the children, then to come between them and their parents so the children felt like they were all alone and unprotected, and then to reveal herself to the parents and scare the family away, psychologically damaged for the rest of their lives. Or she would kill them. She had not yet decided.

Thia could not stand by and watch. She could not let that happen. She had to warn them. So that first night, when Mrs. Choo got in the shower in the servants' quarters, the very one Thia had showered in on her first night, too, Thia rattled the door, just as Winifred had done, hoping to scare Mrs. Choo away.

Just as Thia had done, Mrs. Choo pushed on the door to check for loose hinges.

It was not enough.

Thia slid through the door and touched her finger to the glass, touching a drop of water with her fingertip, testing her ability to interact with the physical world. Carefully, making sure her finger did not go through the door, she slowly wrote "L-E-A-V-E" in the condensation that had settled on the glass.

Mrs. Choo looked on in shock and horror as she watched each letter being formed from *inside* the shower, seemingly from an invisible presence that was right next to her.

She screamed as she pushed the shower door open and started running.

Almost instantly, Winifred was there, her eyes filled with fiery fury. "*What are you doing?*" she yelled at Thia. Then, she grabbed Mrs. Choo by her wet hair and slammed her to the floor.

"What are *you* doing?" Thia screamed.

By then, Mr. Choo had come into the bathroom, his eyes wide with concern. "Are you okay?" he asked his wife, thinking she had slipped and fallen.

To Thia, Winifred said, "I had *plans*. I had grand plans on how I was going to get them to leave, and you *ruined* them!"

Mr. Choo bent down to help his wife stand up, but before

he could get to her, Winifred picked him up and threw him against the opposite wall. Mrs. Choo screamed again as she watched her husband fly across the small room.

"Stop it, Winifred!" Thia yelled. "*Stop it!*"

The older of the two children appeared in the doorway. "What's going on?"

"Run!" Mr. Choo yelled, and the boy disappeared.

Mrs. Choo was on her feet by this time, and Winifred was about to grab her. But Thia stepped in between them and tried to push Winifred away. Mrs. Choo went to her husband's side, and Winifred grabbed the hair dryer, ready to throw it at them. But Thia grabbed it and held on.

Thia said, "That's enough, Winifred. They're leaving. Isn't that what you want?"

The Choos watched in horror as the hair dryer waivered about in the air, seemingly on its own since they could see neither Winifred nor Thia struggling to take control of it.

Without taking his eyes off the hair dryer, Mr. Choo grabbed a towel, held it out toward his wife, and yelled, "Get the kids in the car!"

Mrs. Choo took the towel and wrapped it around herself as she ran out of the bathroom. Mr. Choo followed her, slamming the door shut behind him. Still struggling with the hair dryer, Thia and Winifred heard the dresser being pushed in front of the bathroom door, then the bedroom door being slammed shut, and then the muffled commotion of the family grabbing keys, phones, Mrs. Choo's purse and Mr. Choo's wallet, and telling the kids to leave everything and get to the car.

Thia and Winifred continued to struggle, but Winifred was much stronger than Thia. Then, all of a sudden, seemingly without any effort at all, Winifred took the hair dryer from Thia's grasp and smashed it into the bathroom mirror. Thia flinched as both the hair dryer and the mirror shattered to pieces.

Gliding toward Thia with intimidation and rage, Winifred said cruelly, "This is *my* house. *I* choose who, when, and how people know about us." Thia tried not to cower in fear as Winifred continued, "If you *ever* interfere with my plans again, I won't pretend you have even the slightest chance against me. I will kill them on the spot, right in front of you, and make you watch the consequences of your foolish actions. If you ever do that again, I will *show* you that you can do *nothing* to stop me. Do you understand?"

Thia nodded.

"*Do you understand?*" Winifred asked more forcefully, enunciating each syllable.

Thia answered, "Yes, Winifred, I understand."

UNLIKE THE MORRISONS, THE CHOOS DID NOT return. Shaken by what had happened and Winifred's show of strength, Thia stayed out of her way. She spent most of her time in the servants' quarters because Winifred never went to that part of the house unless she had a good reason, or she helped Millie and Herschel with their duties. At first, she tried to get them to just see or hear her, but she was unsuccessful. Then, gradually, she started working next to them. Eventually, she started talking to them as if they could hear her. It was just so lonely in that house, especially as she avoided Winifred with every turn. And the rest of the property was even lonelier. Millie and Herschel never went to the gatekeeper's house nor the carriage house, and she knew the occasional group of kids or lost hikers might sometimes end up in the forest somewhere on the property, but that was rare and unpredictable. At least Millie and Herschel—and occasionally someone they brought with them—were guaranteed to come at some time during the week.

She could understand why Winifred did not want to cross over completely to the spiritual realm, for her soul was obviously going to Hell. And she understood why Winifred had originally taken up residence at Blairmont Manor, for it was a gorgeous estate. But after only a year there as a ghost, Thia could not understand how Winifred had been there for so long, doing the same thing day after day, lounging in the different sitting rooms, dancing with herself in the ballroom, and listening to that same song on that record, over and over again. Thia could not stand it—the boredom, the monotony, and, most of all, the loneliness.

So one day, when Thia saw Millie reaching for the silver polish on the top shelf, Thia got it down for her. At first, Millie stepped away, obviously terrified. Thia set the plastic container of polish on the table next to her and then slowly slid it toward Millie, letting her know she was not Winifred and that she did not mean her any harm. Millie quickly grabbed it from the table and left without a word. Thia then followed Millie around the house, and that was the day Thia started talking to Millie out loud, even though Millie never indicated she could hear her. Eventually, she started helping her with her chores, such as dusting and vacuuming the hard-to-reach areas. Millie ignored it when things would move on their own, but Thia liked to think that Millie knew it was she who was doing it, as opposed to Winifred, and that Millie was appreciative of the help, just too scared of

Winifred to acknowledge Thia's presence.

Similarly, with Herschel in the gardens, Thia began to pull out the thorny branches so he would not have to risk getting pricked. She helped him lift heavy bags of mulch, and she pulled weeds alongside him. Like Millie, he did not acknowledge her presence, but also like Millie, he never asked her to leave him alone.

They existed this way, peacefully, each in their own little area of the manor, even after the McRoys moved in. Thia stayed out of Winifred's way, and after two weeks, Winifred still had done nothing to any members of the family, which was much longer than it had been for the Morrisons or the Choos. It gave Thia hope that maybe Winifred *was* capable of living peacefully, as long as she was not bothered.

Then, one day she was in the kitchen talking to Millie, when one of the McRoys came in and said to her, "Hello, you must be one of Millie's granddaughters! It's nice to meet you. I'm Jonathan—"

Millie looked at the space Jonathan had addressed and asked, "Is there someone there?"

Millie backed away, and Jonathan looked at her, confused. Looking down at the floor but with her body facing toward the space Jonathan had addressed, Millie said, "I'm doing what I am supposed to do, no more, no less. I'll be out of here when I'm done with today's chores."

Jonathan, still confused, glanced at Thia and then said to Millie, "Millie, it's okay. You don't even work for us. We appreciate what you—"

"I wasn't talking to you," Millie said harshly.

While this was happening, Winifred appeared in the doorway, and Thia gasped. At Thia's reaction, Jonathan turned around and saw Winifred and asked her, "Who are you?"

"Is there someone else there?" Millie asked.

More confused than ever, Jonathan turned to her and said, "Of course there is. Can't you see her?"

"We must go at once," Millie said, heading for the door.

Another human showed up at the entrance to the room behind Winifred.

Addressing both of the humans now, Millie said, "You all have to leave."

In an instant, Winifred was in front of Millie and pushed her backward, causing her to fall to the floor.

The humans rushed to help her, but Winifred shoved them out of the way. Standing over Millie, Winifred said in a throaty, menacing voice that Thia had never heard before, "You will finish your chores."

Still unable to see Winifred but having heard the strange voice, Millie nodded and said, "Yes, Miss."

Confused, Jonathan looked at Thia and asked, "What's going on? Who are you people?"

"What people?" the other human asked, unable to see the ghosts.

"You have to leave!" Thia said urgently.

Winifred said to Thia, "I told you to stay out of my way."

"I haven't done anything!" Thia told her.

"I told you never to reveal yourself first. If the humans are to know we're here, they know about me before they know about you."

"But it was an accident! How was I to know one of them could see me when I've been invisible to them all along? I even ran into one of them in the gardens the other day, and they walked right through me before I had a chance to get away. And it doesn't matter anyway because I haven't *done* anything. They came in here on their own. I didn't mean to show myself or make my—*our*—presence known."

"I told you what would happen if you did this again," Winifred said, grabbing a cleaver from among the knives.

Seemingly knowing what was to come, Millie got up and ran to the exit, yelling to the other humans, "We have to leave now!"

The human who could not see the ghosts backed away from the floating cleaver, while Jonathan asked Winifred, "What are you doing?"

Without warning, Winifred swung the cleaver, too fast for Jonathan to move out of the way.

But Thia was faster. She rushed to that side of the room and stuck her hand out, catching the blade in her grasp just before it decapitated him. She held on to it tightly, the back of her hand pressing against his neck. She was not sure how much longer she could keep the cleaver from passing through her ghostly form. She looked him in the eyes and yelled, *"Run!"*

Jonathan slipped to the side, getting out from under the pressure of Thia's hand and the blade, and together the two humans fled. Winifred started to go after them, but Thia stopped her by pulling her back into the kitchen by the back of her dress.

She freed herself from Thia's grip and went after the humans again. But again, Thia caught up to her and stopped her. They continued like this until Thia was sure enough time had passed that all the humans were safely in their vehicles, down the road, and beyond the town square.

Absolutely furious, her eyes filled with rage, Winifred yelled, *"Do not ever do that again!"*

"Or what," Thia asked, "you'll kill me?"

"Oh, I'll do much worse than that."

Overcome with frustration, Thia floated through the walls to the outside and to the gate. She could not take it any longer. She could not stay there.

She was frustrated and scared and sad, mad at Winifred and mad at her fate. She wanted to scream or cry or do anything to release this torturous amalgam of emotions, but she had no way to express them, these residual remains of her mind that had been separated from their physical counterpart.

With mad fury, Thia flew into the force field at the boundary of the property as fast as she could, hoping to break through it, only to be repelled. She took a step to the side and tried again. She continued, stepping aside and trying again, and then again and again and again. She flew toward the barrier with all her might. There had to be a way out. She would test every square inch of this boundary if she had to.

As she continued along, searching for a hole in that force field, she startled a squirrel that scurried away behind her. She had scared away many of the forest creatures during this mission, but this time, when she heard the squirrel run away, instead of only the swishing sound of the leaves under its paws, she also heard a familiar jingling sound.

She turned to see where the sound was coming from. She went to the area where the squirrel had been. Sure enough, once she used her foot to forcefully step onto it, she heard the bells. She knelt down and shoved away the leaves and branches, and lo and behold, there they were, all the bell collars she had placed on the door handles in the house, with the ribbons still tied to them.

She picked up a few and then, still holding them in her hands, moved more of the leaves and twigs out of the way to reveal all the bell collars.

"Hey, y'all...?" she heard a young boy say. "Those bells are moving on their own."

Thia looked up and saw a group of kids in the near distance. There were five of them, all of whom she recognized, having seen them in town. They were each looking at the bells, the ones still in a pile on the ground and the ones she held suspended in the air. All the children, except one. When Thia looked at her, the little girl was looking directly at Thia's eyes.

"You can see me," Thia whispered. Then, excited, she stood up, the bells in her hands ringing as she did so. She exclaimed, "You can see me!"

All five of the children screamed as they turned and ran toward the town square.

"Wait!" She flew after them, the bells ringing in her hands, until she was forced to stop at the boundary of the property. Watching as they fled, dodging trees and bushes, she yelled after them, "Come back! Please! Tell Dr. Bachmann to tell Dr. Manning I'm still here!" Then she repeated more loudly, "I'm still here!"

But they were too far away to hear her. And even if they could hear her, she was sure they were too scared to comprehend what she was saying.

"I see you found your bells," Winifred said, suddenly next to her.

"It was you all along, wasn't it?" Thia accused her. "*You* made me think there was someone after me. *You* made me think I was mentally unstable." She held the bell collars in her fists up at eye level and shook them. "*You* stood outside the wardrobe and taunted me with these while I was on the phone with 911. And then you hid them so I would question my own sanity."

Winifred grinned and said, "Not bad, eh? I told you this would be fun, once you got to know your humans."

"There is no ghost of Mary Stinson, is there?"

"No, of course not," Winifred said with a smirk. "Souls bound for Heaven go there right away. Except for you for some reason."

"You used her to lure me to the lake. You knew I would be curious because you were in the library when Dr. Manning told me about her. You knew that once I accepted that you were real, I would look for others, too. But there are no other ghosts, are there?"

"No," Winifred answered. "Just us."

"There is no 'us,'" Thia said, determined to figure out how to separate herself from Winifred, one way or another.

14

GIVEN WHAT HAD HAPPENED WITH THE MCROYS AND seeing now that Winifred would retaliate regardless of what Thia's intentions were, whether or not she meant to interfere with Winifred's so-called "plans" for the humans—and figuring that she really had nothing to lose because she was already dead—Thia decided she would do whatever it took to defeat Winifred and protect the humans from her.

So when the next set of humans arrived, Thia intervened at every chance, getting to them before Winifred could and making sure they left unharmed. And then she did that for the next set of humans and then the next after that. It did not always go smoothly, and it was not always ideal, but it was always better than letting Winifred have her way with them. It got to the point where she did not remember how many years had passed since her death or how many humans had moved in and out. All she remembered were the horrific events caused by Winifred, the so-called accidents, the injuries, and the times she scared them on purpose. Thia vowed she would always intervene and protect the humans to the best of her ability for as long as she was trapped there.

Until the day she was summoned.

All of a sudden, out of nowhere, Thia found herself in the

woods at the edge of the property. In that instant, she knew she had not been there the second before, but for her afterlife she could not remember where she had been or what she had been doing just before that moment.

"Are you sure this is where you saw her?" she heard a man ask.

Then she saw them: a man with one of his arms in a cast and sling, the girl she had seen years before with the group of kids, older now but still recognizable, and the sheriff who had come to her house the day after Winifred had terrorized her with the bells.

The girl, now a young teenager, locked eyes with Thia and pointed at her. "There she is! The Bell Lady!"

"*The Bell Lady*?" Thia asked in a whisper, not knowing why the girl had called her that.

The two men turned to look where the girl was pointing but saw nothing.

"Where do you see her?" asked the man with his arm in a cast. The girl started to back away, but he said, "No, you have to stay. We need to know if it's her. Just stand behind me."

"Hi," Thia said to her, waving her hand, but it only made the girl more scared.

"Cynthia Watkins?" the sheriff asked. "Are you there?"

The Bell Lady, Thia thought, remembering how she had accidentally scared the children that day. She dropped to her knees and started clearing away the leaves, twigs, and branches, searching until she found the pile of bell collars. The air had become eerily quiet, and when Thia turned toward them to see if they were still there, she saw the three of them standing completely still. The girl was now hiding behind the man with the sling. The two men were watching the area where she searched, with no animals nor wind to explain the phenomenon they saw of leaves being frantically scattered around.

"Ah ha!" Thia exclaimed as one of her hands felt the familiar object. She lifted the bell collar and shook it in the air, proclaiming, "Yes, I'm here!"

The girl screamed as the two men stumbled backward.

"What does she look like?" the sheriff asked her. "Is she wearing a dress?"

"I promise I won't hurt you," Thia said to her. "Tell them it's me, Thia."

"Yes," the girl said.

"What color is it?" both men asked at the same time.

"White," the girl responded.

"Is she alone?" the sheriff asked.

"Yes," the girl said.

The men relaxed.

"Please, can I go now?" she asked.

"I told you, I won't hurt you," Thia said, trying to reassure her. She could not bear knowing this girl was afraid of her. That anyone would be afraid of her. "Please, don't be scared."

"Y'all can go on," said the sheriff, addressing the other man and the girl but keeping his eyes on the bell collar in the air. "I'll handle it from here."

Thia watched as the girl and the man with his arm in a sling turned and began walking toward the town square.

The sheriff still could not see her. Instead, he looked at the bell collar, suspended in the air, seemingly all on its own. "Ms. Watkins?"

She shook the bells.

He took a step closer, his eyes still on the bells, before

glancing at the ground to see the pile. Addressing the bells in the air, he said, "I just want to get a closer look. Is that okay?"

Thia waved the collar, causing the bells to jingle.

"I'll take that as a 'yes.' Drop the bells to the ground if it's a 'no.'"

Thia shook the collar to show she was continuing to hold the bells in the air.

With more confidence, the sheriff approached the area where she stood, his eyes on the bells in the air the entire time. When he reached her, he knelt down and moved the leaves and twigs, revealing the stash. "Well I'll be damned," he said. "These are the stolen bells, aren't they?"

"Yes!" Thia exclaimed as she knelt down across from him. "Yes, yes, yes! I told you!"

Unable to see or hear her, but noticing how the bells in the air had lowered to the ground in front of him, he guessed where she was and addressed her. "I remember you said you put them on the doors."

Thia wrapped one around her fist and rotated her wrist, replicating the motion of a doorknob being turned to demonstrate how it made the bells jingle.

The sheriff picked up a collar and tried to mimic the movement. "That's pretty clever."

Thia sat down and put her hands in her lap. She could not stop smiling, so overjoyed was she to be communicating with someone, to finally have a friend.

"You know, there's a rumor in town about you, something about a psychic claiming you're trapped here by the other ghost, the one in the blue dress. I won't say her name. Nobody will, for fear of summoning her. But the rumor is that as long as she's here, you can't move on to the spiritual realm. Is that true?"

Thia shook the bells and said, "I think so. That's what the medium said anyway."

"And that you can't leave the property? Unlike the other one?"

Thia shook the bells again. Then, she said, "Here, I'll show you." She got up and floated to the nearby border and then made a show of trying to cross it a few times, the bells abruptly stopping in the air each time she tried to break through the invisible barrier.

"I see," he said, still kneeling over the bells.

She floated back to where he was and sat across from him again.

"Ms. Watkins," the sheriff said, suddenly serious. "Thia. I'm here to ask you—to beg you, really—to please stop whatever it is you are doing to upset the ghost that haunts this house. Please," he said again. Any hint of his usual authoritative sheriff tone was gone. Instead, he sounded like a father, a brother, a husband, a concerned citizen. "She says she won't leave us alone until you back down. She told us to let you know that she is hurting us because of what you're doing here at the house. And she said you know what she is capable of and that she will do it if you continue."

Thia remained motionless, stunned by what she was hearing but more stricken by the anguish in his tone, the desperation and fear she heard in his voice.

He continued, "She's hurt a lot of people. You saw Frank's arm. You saw how scared his daughter is. The truth is, we're all really scared. A few members of the community have already moved out of Daffodil. Please," he pleaded again, near tears, "please, do whatever she wants you to do. For us. We've lived in peace, knowing she was here, for years. It's never been this bad, not in my lifetime."

Thia thought of the man's arm in a cast, imagining what Winifred had done to him, knowing he could not be the only injured member of the community if the whole town was scared.

But more than that, through him Winifred had made her point: even if Thia could prevent Winifred from harming the humans at Blairmont Manor, she was powerless beyond its borders. Winifred could still retaliate—and clearly already had—by harming humans that were out of Thia's reach.

After a long period of silence, the sheriff asked, "Ms. Watkins?"

She jingled the bells slightly to let him know she was still there.

"Please?" he asked. "There's an emergency town hall meeting tonight to discuss this. Can I tell everyone you have given me your word that you will stop whatever it is you are doing?"

She jingled the bells again.

"Is that a yes?" he asked. "I have to be sure. Ring the bells again for 'yes.' Drop them to the ground for 'no.'"

The nervous look of anticipation in his eyes was heartbreaking.

Holding the bell collar up at eye level, Thia shook it to ring the bells.

With a huge sigh of relief, he placed a hand over his heart and said, "Thank you." Then, he said it again. "Thank you."

As he stood up, so did she, and she watched him as he turned to leave. After a few steps, he turned back around to face her, the collar she still held in her hand the only indication she was still there. She lifted it, hugging it to her chest with both hands.

With more genuine sympathy than she had ever seen or heard expressed by anyone, he said, "I'm sorry this happened to you. I wish there was something I could do about it. I really do. I hope you understand how painful it is for me to feel this helpless. I'm sorry I failed you. I'm sorry we all failed you."

"It's not your fault," she said, although she knew he could not hear her. Here was yet one more person Winifred had made feel guilty about her death, when in reality Winifred was the only one who was truly responsible for it.

Thia watched as he turned and walked through the forest toward the road that led back to the town square.

Then, she dropped the bell collar and rushed to the house to find Winifred. As soon as she found her, she asked, "What have you done?"

"Well, I had to reach you somehow," Winifred told her. "You just wouldn't listen to me."

"What about my mom? And the rest of my family? And my friends? What have you done to them?"

Winifred laughed and turned to leave.

"Winifred, answer me!" Thia demanded.

Winifred ignored her.

"Have you harmed them? Because if you have—" Thia began. She no longer cared about her promise to the sheriff. If Winifred had hurt her friends or family, nothing else mattered.

Winifred turned around and answered, "Maybe I have. Maybe I haven't." Then, with seriousness that left no room for doubt, Winifred warned, "But you can be sure that if you ever interfere again, I will track down and torture your mother, every member of your family, and all those pretty little girls you brought to my house, the ones who sat in those ugly chairs on *my* lawn and trampled on *my* grass and who slept in *my* beds. One by one, I will make them each suffer in ways you cannot even comprehend, and I will make sure their lives are so miserable that they will wish they were dead. And if you continue beyond that, I will inflict so much intolerable pain on them that they will kill themselves just to escape it. Have I made myself clear?"

Completely powerless and knowing Winifred was more than capable of carrying out this threat if Thia did not comply, Thia had no other choice but to surrender. Nodding, she said, "Yes, Winifred, you have."

"Good," Winifred said with finality.

Thia stayed where she was for a moment, wanting assurance that Winifred had not already harmed her friends or family and assurance that Winifred would hold up her end of the bargain if Thia held up hers. But Winifred had already physically harmed innocent people, people who had not even come near Blairmont Manor, and Thia feared now that the slightest challenge or provocation would send Winifred into a manic rage that would result in damages far worse than what she had already threatened to do.

Thia thought about her promise to the sheriff and Winifred's new threats against her family and friends. She had to keep her word. She had to figure out how to stay out of Winifred's way. For over a hundred years, the townspeople of Daffodil had lived with the knowledge of Winifred, knowing how to maintain peace in their town. They did the required minimum to keep her pleasant and undisturbed. Carol, Millie, and Herschel did their parts to keep her content. Now Thia had to do her part, too.

15

FOR NEARLY TWO YEARS, NO HUMANS OCCUPIED Blairmont Manor, and Thia began to think the town had finally purchased the estate to make sure it remained vacant.

She spent her time roaming the property, going for floats in the woods, and occasionally staying in the gatekeeper's house. But she mainly stayed in the gardens in the front or to the side of the house, unable to bring herself to go to the lakeside. She had not been able to bear seeing it since learning it was where she had been murdered. If she did go inside the house, she kept to the servants' quarters, or she followed Millie around and helped her with her chores.

Millie, as always, parked under the porte cochere and used only the side entrance next to the kitchen to enter and exit the house, leaving her keys and all her belongings in the car in case she had to leave in a hurry.

Herschel came to tend the grounds, and, as he was elderly, Thia helped him when she could. His grandsons and great-grandsons came with him often. Soon, one of them would have to take over Herschel's duties. Thia wondered if he told them about her. If what the sheriff had said was true, then there was already a rumor in town about her being trapped there. And if what the girl had called her was any indication of what was circulating among the youth, then she already had a nickname. So it was likely they already knew about her, but she made sure not to reveal herself so as not to scare them. She would hate herself if they refused to come back because of something she did. Still, when they were there, Thia stayed close by so she could feel like she was among company, like they were her friends or like she was part of their family.

She did see other people occasionally, sometimes a hiker or a group of hikers who had wandered close to the property. In those times, she would try to scare them to steer them as far away from the house as possible.

It was, for the most part, pleasant, and Thia imagined that she could afterlive like this, as lonely as it was. In time, she began to feel like she could get used to it, like maybe this was not so bad after all.

But then the moving truck appeared, and all the trauma flooded back into her mind. She thought of all the incidents, all the suffering Winifred had caused over the years, not only since she had lived in the house but even before that, and she was not sure if she could go through it again. Even if she stayed out of the way—out of the house even—she was not sure she could afterlive with the agony of not being able to warn the family or protect them, afterliving each second in fearful anticipation of the moment when they would make Winifred mad enough to retaliate and inflict irreparable harm.

She realized, then, that it would never be over. As long as Winifred was in that house, Thia would be trapped there. And while this little reprieve had been nice, it almost made things worse as she felt everything crashing down around her, as she felt hopeless and full of despair and dread for what was to come.

She stayed out of the way, as she had promised she would, so as not to accidentally be seen or heard. She did everything she could to distract herself from thinking about the humans in that house with Winifred, occupying her thoughts with anything other than what she imagined might be happening.

But despite her efforts, she had seen the new inhabitants on occasion. They were a family of four: a mother, a father, and their two defiant and rebellious teenage sons. The de la Cruz family was loud and vigorous in their words with each other. Their fights were so loud she could not help but overhear them. The boys would accuse their parents of going into their rooms. The parents yelled at their sons for moving things around or pranking them in the middle of the night. They all blamed each other. Only Thia knew the real cause.

Then, one day she heard them having one of their epic fights, screaming at each other on the veranda. The boys were moving their rooms to the servants' quarters, adamant that the house was haunted, claiming the ghost had told them that they would be left alone if they stayed in the servants' areas. The parents yelled back at them, telling them not to make up stories, telling them they were sick of their lies and wild imaginations. The sons were so angry that veins were popping out in their faces and necks. Their eyes were nearly in tears from their frustration for not being believed.

"*How are you so stupid that you can't see her?*" one of the boys yelled at Mrs. de la Cruz.

"You will *not* talk to your mother that way!" Mr. de la Cruz admonished him.

They continued to fight, and Thia watched from the front garden, slowly creeping closer without realizing she was doing so until a figure in a window caught her eye. She looked up to see Winifred watching her. Slowly, Thia retreated so as not to accidentally be seen by the humans. Winifred gave her a knowing smile of victory. Just as she had planned to do with the Choos, Winifred had come between the children and the parents of the de la Cruz family.

Too disgusted with Winifred to continue looking at her, Thia turned her attention back to the family fighting on the veranda. But more than that, she focused on her own desperate situation. She could not do this. She could not simply stay out of the way, knowing this was happening. And even if she intervened now and scared the de la Cruzes away, others would come, and the cycle would start anew.

Over the last two years, she had fantasized that years from now—fifty or a hundred at least, long after she was sure her friends and family had died—she would somehow defeat Winifred or finally convince her to either move on fully to the spiritual realm or move to another physical location on Earth. But she understood now how impossible that would be. She could not sit by for fifty years doing nothing. She could not afterlive like that. She had to do *something*.

But she also knew she was much weaker than Winifred was. All the times she had been able to intervene, she had not been able to overcome Winifred's strength. All she had been able to do was to get the humans to leave before too much damage was done. They had not always escaped unharmed or unscathed. No, if she were to ever succeed in defeating Winifred, she would need help. She could not do it alone.

The de la Cruzes were forceful and feisty. They fought fiercely with each other, but Thia knew they would be even stronger and more impassioned fighting as a group against a common enemy. She could not take on Winifred alone, but maybe the five of them could.

So that night, she entered the house for the first time since the de la Cruzes had moved in. Knowing the sons were in the servants' quarters, she headed for the bedrooms in the main part of the house. She would start with the parents, she had decided, and then she would go to the sons.

She found Mr. and Mrs. de la Cruz sleeping in what she had named the "Opal Room" when she was alive. She carefully entered, staying vigilant for any signs of Winifred, and floated to the side of the bed where Mrs. de la Cruz was sleeping on her back. Then, Thia placed her hands around the woman's neck and squeezed, careful to apply enough force to strangle her without her hands slipping through the woman's body.

Within seconds, Mrs. de la Cruz opened her eyes, having been awakened by her inability to breathe. Thia felt her neck jerking in her grip as the woman tried to gasp for air. As she began to lose consciousness, her eyes shifted from staring at the ceiling to now meeting Thia's eyes, finally able to see her. Her eyes widened with fear as Thia came into focus. She grabbed at Thia's hands around her neck, only to feel her fingernails scratching her own skin as her fingers slid through Thia's ghostly form.

Mr. de la Cruz was sleeping on his side a couple feet away, with his back turned to his wife. Mrs. de la Cruz reached across the bed, clenched her husband's shirt in her fist, and pulled on it. When he did not wake up, she began hitting his back. Startled, he quickly turned around. Upon seeing her struggling to breathe, he sat up and moved to her side of the bed.

"Angel?" he asked.

Mrs. de la Cruz, unable to move her neck, averted her eyes from Thia and looked at her husband, tears forming in her eyes, her body writhing as she tried to get out of Thia's grip, an awful croaking sound accompanying her every attempt to breathe.

"Angel!" he screamed.

Angel, Thia thought, *so fitting.* She was Thia's angel. They were all her angels. They would help her.

A sudden gag reflex led to a gurgling sound that accompanied the fluid Thia felt filling the woman's throat.

Mr. de la Cruz got his cell phone from the nightstand and dialed 911.

Just a couple more minutes, Thia thought. She would tell them, once they were ghosts, too, about why she had done this and how they would help her. Then, they could all move on to the spiritual realm after they got rid of Winifred. The de la Cruzes would understand. They would forgive her once they met Winifred and saw for themselves how evil she was.

Then, Thia heard that familiar low, rumbling, hollow laughter.

In a flash, she remembered standing by the gate, watching the Choos, declaring that she would never be like Winifred.

Immediately, Thia released her grip and backed away.

Mrs. de la Cruz inhaled sharply as she tried to sit up but was unable to, having not yet fully regained consciousness. She rolled over so that her head was hanging over the side of the bed as she heaved, the fluid that had accumulated in her mouth and throat dripping off her lips and onto the floor. Mr. de la Cruz rushed to her side as he continued to tell the 911 dispatcher what was happening. Mrs. de la Cruz looked up, not at her husband but at the location where Thia had been.

Thia, realizing neither of the de la Cruzes could see her now, started backing away.

"Oh come on," Winifred said. "You're not leaving, are you? You were so close!" Laughing, she said, "I was so proud of you! You can't stop now!"

Horrified by her own behavior, Thia rushed out of the house, with Winifred remaining in the room, laughing and laughing and laughing.

She floated as far away from the house as she could get, clear on the other side of the property, devastated by what she had done.

Although her intentions had been good, she now knew for herself that, given the right circumstances, the potential to act evil exists in each of us. She had allowed herself to be so affected that she behaved in a way of which she would have never before believed herself capable. She had become unrecognizable to herself, and she vowed right then and there to never let herself reach that point ever again.

To that end, she knew she could never go back to the house; she was now exiled to the woods.

FOR DAYS, THIA STAYED AT THE OTHER SIDE OF THE property, unable to bring herself to return to the mansion. She wallowed in self-pity, consumed by thoughts of her miserable situation. She could not leave the property. She could not overpower Winifred or make her leave. She could not interfere with Winifred's wickedness without risking retaliation. And now she knew she could not sit by and do nothing.

It was a hard lesson for Thia to learn but one that she finally did, that we must live—and die—by the decisions we make. Thia had chosen to ignore the signs, had chosen to be in denial of such evil deception existing, and in doing so she had made the choice to let Winifred put her in the position in which she now found herself.

She thought about her mother, her family, her friends, all of whom she missed so dearly. She thought about her life, her dreams, everything she had worked for, everything she had accomplished. She thought about her actual, physical life. All of it had been snatched away from her by that wretched beast of a ghost Winifred.

She thought about the sheriff, the medium, the kids, and the girl and her father. They all knew she was there. The whole town probably knew by now, but nobody would ever come to visit her, not that she could blame them. Thia would never want anyone to risk crossing paths with Winifred.

Thus, Winifred had also taken from her even the possibility of friends and companionship. Because of Winifred, she would forever be alone. Because of Winifred, she had nothing.

Except the bells.

Thia somberly made her way to that area of the forest and found the stash of bell collars.

Picking one up, she realized these were all that remained of the beautiful life she had once created for herself—these bells that were purchased to give her peace of mind but which were instead used to create mental turmoil as they were stolen from her and hidden here by the fiend who played with her sanity for amusement.

She remembered how these collars had scared the children, how the men had stumbled backward in fear upon seeing one suspended in the air by itself. She remembered seeing hikers in the woods and trying to scare them away before Winifred found out about them and decided to scare them away herself. How much easier that would have been if she'd had these bells!

Then, she slowly twisted the collar around in her hand as she envisioned doing that now, keeping people away from harm by scaring them away. Perhaps these bells could be used for good after all. She could use them to prevent lost hikers or others who just didn't know better from getting too close.

She thought about what the sheriff had said, about how Winifred had never been this bad in his lifetime. Left to herself, Winifred harmed no one. She existed in the house, listening to her record, dancing her waltz, doing whatever she did to occupy her time. It was only when people—or Thia—got in her way that she became ornery and vengeful. As long as she was left alone, the townspeople would not even know if she was still there. Thus, she always held control over them, for even in times of peace the people of Daffodil still lived in fear, not knowing if it was peaceful because Winifred was gone or because she was content.

But Thia could let them know. They knew she was trapped there by Winifred. She was sure the sheriff had told the town at the emergency meeting. So they knew if she was still there, then Winifred was, too. With her bells, she could let the townspeople know in times of peace that they still needed to stay away, that these woods were still not safe. As long as she kept her distance from the house, she would be out of Winifred's way. And Winifred would be satisfied because this would be yet one more measure to make sure she was not disturbed.

A wave of tranquility flowed through her with the thought, and for the first time since her death she felt calm and at peace. Even in tragedy, joy can be found in finding purpose for one's existence. This was something she could *do*, an *action* she could take. *This* was something she could afterlive for. *This* would give her afterlife meaning.

With one last look at the mansion in the distance, she knew she would never see the inside of it ever again. Her place was no longer in that house; her place was now in these woods. One by one, she fastened the collars around her wrists and ankles. Then, she started walking, moving her arms and legs so all the bells would jingle in a rhythmic—intentional—way, an obvious warning signal to anyone who might hear it.

To this day, those who dare to get close enough can hear her in that forest. She patrols the grounds, ringing her bells so the townspeople will know the mansion is still haunted by pure evil. And if anyone should ever wander into those woods, they can only hope she reaches them before Winifred even knows they are there.

THE END

Acknowledgements

This book would not have been possible without the countless hours and effort of a wonderful editor. Thank you for your thoughtful consideration of every detail and working with me to make *The Bell Lady of Blairmont Manor* the ghost story it is today.

To Hannah Linder, thank you for such a beautiful cover. Thank you, especially, for your patience, your talent, and your brilliant ideas. It was a pleasure to work with you.

To my friends and family, thank you for all your love, acceptance, and support over the years. It means the world to me, and I truly hope I have been successful in returning the sentiment.

About the Author

Novella Jean grew up in Nashville, TN, and, after some short stays in Texas and Oregon, now lives in Washington State with her husband and their cat. *The Bell Lady of Blairmont Manor* is her first horror novel. She is also the author of the satire novelette *Rita, Riley, and 'Rona Anxiety*.

Post-Credits Scene

FROM HER POSITION IN THE WOODS, THIA COULD SEE the lights of the house. She could even hear the low murmur of many voices chatting at once, with the occasional exclamation of loud laughter or a greeting. Halloween was usually her busiest night, especially since more families had moved to the area and teens were becoming more daring, particularly on this holiday. Some came with eggs to throw or spirit boards and planchettes. Most came with skepticism. Thia always came with her bells, scaring them off, away from Winifred and back to safety.

This year, however, the new owners of Blairmont Manor were throwing a party, and as Thia saw more cars enter through the open gate, her curiosity grew. She floated closer to the house, to the edge of the clearing where the lawn met the forest. Orange and purple lights adorned the front veranda. Decorations of webs with spiders were in the bushes. One decoration, affixed to the side of the house, looked like a witch had crashed into it on her broom. Thia's favorites were, naturally, the ghosts hanging in the trees.

Adults of all ages had parked in the grass to keep the driveway clear. Winifred would never tolerate that. But Winifred would also never tolerate a party of this magnitude.

Thia started to remove her bells. Over the years— whether driven by superstition or curiosity or gratitude, she did not know—people left bells at the edge of the property for her, not only collar bells but bells of all shapes and sizes.

She added her favorites to the collection she carried. So many did she have now that she no longer needed to purposely shake them, for they jingled on their own with only the slightest movement on her part before one would hit another and then another and so on until they were all ringing in their own little ways with unique sounds to create a chaotic, metallic noise.

She slid the final bells off of herself and left them next to a tree. She told herself she was just getting a closer look, just checking to see what was going on, barely allowing herself to scarcely hope that Winifred was somehow no longer there. At the very least, she had not yet revealed herself to the new owners. Otherwise, they never would have thrown a party like this one, with so many guests.

She did not know who these owners were. Over the years, she stopped keeping track. Someone would buy Blairmont Manor and move in. Soon after that, the house would be abandoned. Carol would show up with potential buyers, and one of them would put an offer on the house, despite her best efforts to persuade them to keep looking. They would move in, then move out. Carol would show up with someone new, and the cycle would continue.

For self-preservation, for what little self she had left to preserve, Thia had to stop watching. She could do nothing about it, and it would send her into despair every time she saw a moving truck. So, she focused on what she could do. She patrolled the woods and rang her bells whenever someone came near. And if they did not heed the warning of her bells, she scared them away by other means. To most, seeing bells ringing by themselves, suspended in the air, was terrifying enough. Most could not see her. But occasionally, very rarely over the years, one person would see her, go pale with momentary shock, and then come back to their senses and run away. She took no amusement from it, only the satisfaction in knowing they were running away from the real danger and that she had prevented them from coming to any harm.

If Winifred was ever annoyed or entertained by her activity in the woods, she never let on either way. They had not spoken since the night Thia left, the night she had almost murdered Mrs. de la Cruz. Their last interaction was one of Thia in stark terror of her own actions and Winifred laughing hysterically.

They seemed to have informally reached an understanding, whereby Thia, unable to leave the property, remained outside, and Winifred, free to go wherever she pleased, remained inside. As long as Thia stayed out of her way, it seemed that Winifred did not care who saw her or heard her bells.

But with the house like this now, full of people, could it be that Winifred was no longer there? Dare Thia even begin to entertain the notion that someone might have been able to get her to move on, either to another physical location on Earth or to cross over fully to the spiritual realm?

Thia went through the side gardens and around to the back. Night had fallen, and the full moon hung in the sky almost directly above the lake. It was a view she never thought she would tire of when she was alive. Now, it was a view she could not bear to face. The location of her death on its anniversary looked so similar to how it had on that fateful night. It was a painful reminder of what a fool she had been—to believe Mary Stinson's ghost could still be there, to believe she and Winifred could be friends, to believe Winifred could be anything other than the malevolent spirit that she was and forever would be.

Avoiding looking at the lake, Thia focused on the guests and the decor. Every detail was perfect, exactly as she had wanted it to be when she was alive. There were chairs and tables in the little alcoves of the gardens. Small groups of guests dressed in Halloween costumes were sipping wine and cocktails among the stringed lights and decorations.

Thia dared to get a little closer, carefully observing the humans to see if anyone was looking at her. While she was sure she was dressed for the occasion—she was still wearing her Juliet costume—she was certain she was transparent or had some ghost-like appearance because Winifred always had a semitransparent look about her. But for all Thia knew, that was yet one more thing Winifred knew how to control that she did not.

Nobody seemed to notice her, either because she was invisible to them or because she looked like a guest. She took a few more steps toward the house, feeling the excitement of the party now and loving every moment of it. When she was alive, she had wanted to host a party like this one—many parties like this one—and this was exactly how she would have done it. Dare she dream, even for just half a moment, that Winifred was not here? That all this might finally be over? That the house had at last been able to get what it deserved, to be an architectural marvel full of happy people enjoying its remarkable beauty?

She relaxed and glided among the living more freely, careful not to run into anyone or touch anything, lest she knock something over and startle someone—or accidentally possess one of the humans. She laughed with one group when someone in a funny costume arrived. She agreed when one group commented on how beautiful the decorations were. She said, "No thank you," when a server with a tray of champagne offered the person standing next to her a drink, as if they had been speaking to her. She allowed herself to pretend this was a party being hosted at her luxury boutique hotel. These were the guests of her clients, who had rented Blairmont for the evening and booked all the rooms for the night. She would have circulated among the guests like this to ensure everyone was enjoying themselves. She would have been in and out of the kitchen and checking with the serving staff to make sure the event was running smoothly.

And, of course, she would have checked with the clients, the couple who had rented the venue to host this elaborate party. Through her time in the garden, she had eavesdropped enough to piece things together. This was not only a Halloween party, it was a Halloween-themed housewarming party. The young couple, a husband and wife in their late twenties, was recently married; at least one guest expected the bride to be pregnant soon, if she was not already; and the house was a wedding gift from the bride's mother, a foreign billionaire of some sort.

Thia crossed the patio and approached the back entrance, and that was when her enchanted evening came to a screeching halt. Through the window, she saw that the interior was the same as when she had lived there. Seeing it, a flood of traumatic memories came back to her, from when she was alive and naive and since she had become a ghost.

Winifred still haunted the house.

Of course she's still here, Thia thought. *Otherwise, I wouldn't be here.*

But Winifred was not harming anyone tonight.

At least not yet.

Thia crossed the threshold and entered the house. She

wanted to reminisce, to continue the dream that she was alive, that she was somehow connected to this party full of so many happy people and friends. She wanted to enjoy the beauty of the house and the exquisite furniture that was still so fitting and impressive.

But all she could see were reminders of horrible events. There was the chair Winifred had thrown that broke a painter's arm. There was the wall from which Winifred had emerged to scare one of the human inhabitants. There were reminders everywhere.

Where she did not see reminders, she saw potential disasters or props for Winifred to use. The bone china, the serving knives, every glass and utensil—even some of the costumes could be used as weapons. And as for the costumes that covered a body from head to toe, one of them could be Winifred, for all Thia knew.

She reached the grand entryway at the front of the house. She had never appreciated just how large and heavy the chandelier appeared, nor how lofty that second floor overlook was and how far one would fall if they were pushed over the railing. The two-story windows on either side of the large wooden double doors had the most incredible curtains Thia had ever seen. She remembered being astounded the first time she saw them, even though she had only been able to give them a cursory glance as Carol rushed her out of the house. Now, she only saw the ropes that were used to pull them back, how they looked sturdy enough to hold a hanging body that would swing from side to side in front of the window. So much psychological damage Winifred could cause tonight. So many deep emotional scars she could make.

But that was not Winifred's way. Winifred preferred to play with her prey, playing with their minds, emotions, and sanity. That had to be Winifred's plan, Thia was sure, to let this party take place so the newlyweds would feel safe and secure. Then she could torture them and make them psychologically pay for this wrongdoing of having so many people invading her home—not that Winifred was incapable of causing a disaster, it was just not her preferred method. As long as she was not backed into a corner, as long as she had no reason to retaliate, Winifred would harm no one tonight. Instead, she would use this event as an opportunity to gather information that she could later use against her new housemates in a long, drawn-out game of driving them mad, as she had done to Thia.

Thia knew she was using these thoughts to rationalize her decision to remain in the house. Thinking Winifred would do nothing tonight helped Thia relax, and she tried once more to fit in, to *be* at the party.

She went past the chair and table her mother had loved so much and entered one of the sitting rooms. In a corner, two older women were sitting and talking, champagne in hand. With one glance at their body language, Thia could tell they had been lifelong best friends. Their costumes were the bare minimum to get by. One woman wore black pants, a black shirt, and black cat ears on a headband. The other woman wore a pantsuit and a bright pink cone-shaped princess hat with a long veil coming out of the point at the top.

The chairs they were sitting in had been moved, and Thia resisted the urge to put them back to where Winifred wanted them to be. Instead of being three in a row, side by side along one wall, they were positioned in a corner, facing each other to form a semicircle. The two ladies were sitting in the chairs across from each other, so Thia slipped between them and sat in the one in the middle. She held her hand in the air, as if also holding a glass of champagne, and pretended to be part of their conversation.

As they spoke, Thia learned that they were old friends of the groom's mother and had known the groom since birth. They talked about some gossip, about the young couple, about how they loved the bride, and about how beautiful and perfect the house was. Thia nodded in agreement and took a pretend sip of her pretend champagne.

"To be young and in love and in your twenties again…" the princess said.

The woman with cat ears said, "And to live in this house!"

The women laughed, and Thia smiled. It *had been* wonderful to be in her twenties in this house, so full of potential and hope, her whole life and new business ahead of her. The possibilities had been endless back then.

Then the princess posed the question, "If you could go back in time to when you were their age, what advice would you give yourself?"

Without hesitation, Thia replied, "Never try to befriend a ghost."

Cat ears turned her head in Thia's direction and looked at the chair she was sitting in.

"What is it?" the princess asked, startled by her friend's sudden interest in the empty chair.

"Didn't you hear that?" cat ears asked.

"Hear what?"

"I heard someone talking," cat ears said with certainty that indicated to Thia that she was not about to let anybody tell her she was at all mistaken. As she lifted her hand and held it over the chair, Thia anticipated in horror as the woman nearly touched her ghostly form. With her fingers outstretched, as if pointing with her palm, she stated, "Right here."

Thia remained completely still, hoping beyond hope that the women would laugh it off and move on, that they would forget about it and that, most importantly, they would keep this little incident to themselves.

It is Halloween, after all, Thia rationalized in her mind. *So even if they tell someone, others will assume it's a prank or that they've had too much to drink and are just caught up in the spirit of the holiday, right?*

Thia looked at each of the women with a newfound hope that nothing would come of this and a new vow to herself to stay completely silent for the rest of the evening.

Suddenly, it was as if the whole world around her became a blur. Thia looked straight ahead and immediately locked eyes with the only costumed figure in focus. Standing on the other side of the room was that familiar sinister glare, so cold and chilling it was as if those eyes would literally freeze whatever they gazed upon and turn it into solid ice. Winifred was in costume, unrecognizable from head to toe, but Thia knew those eyes.

Then, Winifred's expression softened. There was a glint of excitement in her eyes now. She tilted her head to the side, and Thia knew that behind her mask Winifred's lips were slowly spreading to form a cunning smile. It was a look Thia knew all too well, one that sent tremendous fear and dread throughout her core. It was that deceitful look of Winifred's, that one she had used to convince Thia they could coexist in the house when she was alive, that look which portrayed kindness and understanding, and maybe even forgiveness.

But Thia knew better than to think anything other than her worst nightmare was about to ensue. Winifred did not like it when Thia interfered with her plans.